CHANDLER

BISHOP'S SNOWY LEAP BOOK 2

KATHI S. BARTON

World Castle Publishing, LLC
Pensacola, Florida

Paperback ISBN: 9781951642488
eBook ISBN: 9781951642495
First Edition World Castle Publishing, LLC, March 9, 2020
http://www.worldcastlepublishing.com

Licensing Notes

Cover: Karen Fuller
Editor: Maxine Bringenberg

Chapter 1

Sasha got back to her rental and sat down at the table. The dead woman knew her. The place was furnished, thankfully, so she didn't have to worry about anything other than food. The dead woman in the field knew her. Sasha would have to make dinner soon. Looking around the kitchen area, she wondered how she'd gotten home. Her mind wouldn't be still long enough for her to focus on one thing for more than a second or two.

Laying her head down on the table, she thought about the things that the woman, Melinda Harvard, had told her. Not just that, she needed to be found—they knew where she was—but about not just her death, but the baby too. Also, she was her sister, she'd told her. Sasha didn't know what to think about her saying that. As far as she knew, she had just the one sister, and she didn't look like Melinda at all. She didn't even act like her.

While Pearl still lived at home, taking care of their mom, she'd never been as thin as she wanted to be. Pearl had weighed close to four hundred pounds the last time she'd seen her, over three years ago now. Sasha, too, had always had to fight with her weight. But she wasn't obese, or anything like her sister was. Sasha made sure that she kept up with her exercise program. And when she wasn't able to run or something like that, she'd go to the gym.

Melinda had been thin, but it seemed more like she was just that way, rather than she'd had to work at it. Sasha had no idea why that mattered, but she was trying to think of things that would make what the woman had told her true. Which, Sasha realized, was more than likely just that. Just as true as Sasha being able to talk to ghosts.

In thinking of her sister, she thought of her mom. Her mother was a liar and a thief. She scammed people when she could, even if there was no reason for her to do so. Sasha also knew that her mom could get up and around as well as Sasha could. Being confined to a wheelchair, as she told everyone, was a bald faced lie, like most of the things that spewed from her mother's lips—like her name.

Her mom had been calling herself Katie since Sasha

had been a child. Her real name was Sally, but she had always liked the name Katie and decided that it made her sound younger. Sasha had never understood her mother—even less, her brother and sister. Her dad was the only one that not only believed in her but gave her shelter when talking to the dead got to be too much. With her parents divorced since she'd been five, it was easier to stay away from Katie when she got it into her head that Sasha needed to be doing more for her.

Sasha got up to make herself a cup of tea, her mind still battling with the things she'd been told. The brewing of the tea, the putting in the sugar and lemon, gave her something else to think about, even if momentarily.

As soon as she sat down, Sasha thought of Melinda. She'd gone to the body to see if she could find out who had killed the woman and left a newborn behind. Sasha liked the big ex-cop who had been there and didn't mind helping him out when he'd ask. Sasha knew something was off almost before she got to the body. The ghost was staring at her with a huge smile.

"There you are." Sasha told her that she didn't know her. "No, but I do you. You're my sister. My older sister by five years. Your mother, our mother, gave me away when she figured that people would think her much too old to have another child. Since they knew who she was, they put my name on the birth certificate as well as hers. That way, I was able to find you."

"I have a sister and a brother." Melinda had told her their names and their birthdates. "That's correct. Why are you here? I don't usually get to— Do you know who murdered you?"

"I do." She looked at Sawyer then, and the man that was standing nearby, a cop whose name she couldn't remember. "It's not like you think, whatever you're thinking. I wasn't killed by any of those that we're related to. I don't know why I cannot think of his name, but you don't know him."

"I don't usually come to people where they've been killed or died. The dead usually seek me out, and I tell someone where they are to be found. This is all new to me." Melinda said that she'd been given permission to talk to her. "By whom? There are more people out there like me?"

"Yes. Very many like you are now. But that is to change. You'll need to start helping us." Melinda sat down beside her or made it look like she was sitting. "You've been so very helpful to the dead, sister mine. You've helped so many of us find peace, and given those that we love more peace in that bodies have been found and put to rest. We cannot thank you enough for that."

"I didn't have a choice in the matter. They just started coming to me when I was four. I haven't any idea why I can even do this shit." Melinda asked her about the mark that was on the bottom of her left foot. "So? I've had that forever. It's even noted on my baby chart that I have it. What is it other than a birthmark?"

"A mark of birth." Sasha told her that she didn't know what she meant. "You were hurt in the womb, and that made you so much different than other children being born. Others like you need to be taught how to do what you do naturally. My child, my daughter, has the same marking. The man who murdered me, he thought he was killing you or someone that could talk to ghosts. He wishes us dead so that we will not tell anyone what he's done. I still don't know his name, but as I said, you know him."

"Was he going to kill the baby? Your child?" Melinda watched as pictures were taken of her body. When she was flipped to her back, Sasha could see that her belly had been cut open, the child taken from her. "He did this to you?"

"No. He only shot me, in my belly there where I've cut myself. I did the rest. I could not let her die within me. I needed her to be found, and someone—someone like you—to raise her. To keep her safe." Sasha told her that she didn't want a child. "Then she will die as well, I think. He will find her through records."

"Sasha?" She looked at Sawyer when he said her name. "We know that you're speaking to her. What we don't know is what's going on. Can you tell us anything about her murderer? Did he do this to her?"

Sasha told him about how Melinda had delivered her own child. That the man had meant to kill them both after he realized it wasn't Sasha. That he wanted them both dead. However, she didn't tell him that they were related. Nor did she mention that she was supposed to take the child to raise as her own.

"You will need his help, they told me. The Bishop men are worthy of one, such as yourself. They are well respected on both sides of this sphere." Sasha asked her who had told her that. "The dead. Those in charge of making sure that the rules of our kind are enforced. That we're doing nothing to the living, nor are we harming those that helped us be found. There are others out there that do more. You will never have to do what they do. But you will be the one that they go to when they have unsolved business to take care of, such as finding the person or people that killed them. You have been, I guess, promoted."

"Promoted? I don't want to be promoted, damn it. I want to just do what I do and nothing more." Melinda started to fade. "I have so many questions. You can't leave me yet."

"I must, I'm afraid. I have lingered too long on this sphere." She stood up when Melinda began to fade more. "His first name begins with the letter 'C'—that is all that I can remember. You must find him before he finds you. He will know when my death is announced, that he killed the wrong person."

Then she was gone. Sasha had come back home in a fog, not letting her mind think of anything but the next step to getting there—get in the car, start the car, and things such as that. Now here she sat with so much useless information that she didn't know where to even start.

Sitting at the table, stirring her tea until it was cool enough to drink, she got herself a pen and paper and began writing down all the people that she knew whose first name began with the letter C. There was a pitiful number of them, and only a scant few of them even knew what she did for others.

Not sure what she was supposed to do now, she picked up her tea and dumped it into the sink. Sasha didn't even care for the drink, but there was something so calming about making it that she kept the bags around just for the simple pleasure of making it.

When her cell phone rang, she picked it up after seeing the face of her mom. Sitting down again, she was ready for the battle that would ensue. Deciding not to talk about what she'd discovered today, she made sure that her mom knew that she was busy upon answering the phone.

"I don't care what you might think you're doing

that makes you too busy to talk to me. Where have you been, Sasha? I've been by your apartment several times, and you're not there. I want to know what you're up to now." Sasha laid her head back on the table when she saw that Hailey had returned. "Are you there? It would be just like you to just put the phone down and not speak to me."

"I'm here. I have had a rough morning already, and I don't want to have to deal with whatever drama you think you might have going on in your life at the moment. Also, how the hell did you go by my house, Mom? I thought that you weren't to drive. You *said* you couldn't walk." That didn't sit well with her mom, but she didn't care. "Whatever you've done, whatever you've had done to you, it's not my concern. You got yourself into whatever mess you're in, get yourself out of it."

"When did you become so horrid, Sasha? You used to be such a fun loving little girl. Where did she go?" Not answering her didn't seem to be an option with her mom today. "Tell me what it is so that I can tell you to get over it and—"

"I grew up and figured out that you're not as young, as nice, or as wonderful as you and your clique thinks you are. You're a mean, hateful person that thinks revenge is the only way that you can make people pay for whatever shit you're doing at the moment that goes belly up." Mom huffed at her. "As I said, I have things going on here, and I need to get to them. Call Pearl or Zack home. They'll be rooting you on in your misdeeds because they don't know you the way I do."

Disconnecting the call made her feel better, but not for long. Looking at Hailey when she moved to stand in front of her, Sasha asked her what she needed. The smile that she gave her was watery, with bits of underwater things hanging out. Sasha shivered.

"I've been found, thanks to you." Sasha asked her why she was still here then. "I've been asked to keep an eye on you. To help you with your new job."

"I don't remember saying that I'd take it. Besides, if it's just more of the same, I've learned it by myself. I'm sure that I can figure out the rest. Don't you?" Hailey began to change. Not fade, but to become what she might have looked like before her untimely death. "You'll be human again?"

"No. Not human. I thought that it would be much easier for you to see me like this, rather than how I looked when they pulled me from the water this afternoon. You did very well with the Bishop person today. He will be an ally for us both. He and his family." Sasha pointed out that she worked alone and liked it that way. "You have done very well in the past, Sasha, but things needed to change. In that, you were the one that was chosen to help more people. It will be good for us."

"And what about me? How is this going to be better for me? Did anyone think about how much I've given up to help the dead? How very little sleep I get when you and the others come to me in the middle of the night and then bug me until you're found? Did anyone mention that?" She asked Sasha if not being able to sleep would have mattered in the long run. "Yes, it would have mattered. I can't hold down a job. And the little work that I do get, someone always comes along and screws that up for me too. I'm broke. The last of my money was used to come here. Because you dragged me here by telling me how important it was that I help them find you. I did that."

"You did. Would you like to know why it was so important?" Sasha said that she didn't care. Hailey just smiled as she spoke again. "Bradley was planning the same demise for the woman that he is living with now. She deceived him by not telling him of her children, of which she has three. They, too, would have been murdered. Her youngest child, Beth, is to become a great attorney someday. Someone that will fight for the dead and their rights. There are none of those now."

"This is the reason that I don't want to know shit about those that I have to help." Sasha paced the room as Hailey waited. "This 'C' person. Does he really exist? Is he really going to come after me? And that little baby?"

"Yes. He will kill you both if he finds you." Sasha didn't care about herself, but it would hurt her if something happened to her...niece, she supposed. "The babe is in good hands now. She is being called Pip. There is no other name for her that we were told. The man that is caring for her, he is as good a man, as is his brother, the cop that you worked with today. You will need them all, especially this man, when the man comes for you."

"This is a fucked up nightmare. You know that, don't you?" Hailey told her how sorry she was. "I'm sorry too. This isn't your fault. It's mine, for thinking I could ever have a normal life."

Before she changed her mind about this, even if she'd had a choice, she pulled out the business card that had been given to her by Sawyer. Calling the man to see how she could get help from him, she told him that she'd like to meet him at his house. She figured that was the best way to figure out what the fuck was going to happen to her now. Also, she told him that she'd need a ride to and from his home, please?

~*~

Raven watched the proceedings of her mother's pretrial hearing. Not only had she been found to be quite sane, which no one that had met her believed, but they thought that she was competent to stand trial for her crimes. Not that Mother thought she'd done anything wrong, but she had killed her entire family as a child, and that was what they were going to try her for. She had also murdered several people recently in the name of getting things to impress her clique at the club. And she'd kidnapped Raven's daughter, Molly, and nearly killed her.

The people there were listening intently to what was going on. Most of them, Raven had found out, had been taken advantage of in some way. Whether it was financial or physically, Merriam Addington had been worse than any of them had thought. Including her father.

Roger, her dad, was getting on with his life now that his wife of thirty years was no longer bullying him around. And Mother had been a bully, too. She didn't even care if she had to lie or cheat to get him to do what she told him. The thing that bothered the family was that Mother had thought she was the first and only Addington, and that other Addingtons were to use her as a guide on how to act and live. The fact that her only daughter had a child out of wedlock made her feel that Molly wasn't a real person and that she should have been killed at all costs.

Raven had been an adult when she had Molly. The man that she'd been having a fling with had already been married, which Raven hadn't known about. Then a few weeks after she broke it off with him, he'd been killed, which Raven thought had worked out well for her and Molly. His plan had been to marry her after killing off his current wife, then to kill Raven. After that, he'd be wealthy—her name and money would open doors for him. Mostly to the bars, but they'd be opened up.

"Mrs. Bishop? Would you mind coming forward, please?" Raven stood up and made her way to the dais that the judge was sitting behind. Something must have happened, she supposed, while she'd been thinking because he looked about as stressed as any man that she'd ever seen. "Your mother would like to have a word with you about her living conditions."

Raven glanced at her mother before looking at the judge with a smile. "No. I like her right where she is." The judge glanced at his name bar to remind her to address him properly, and Raven told Judge Henry that she was sorry. He rubbed his hand over his face to the back of his hair. It looked as if he'd been doing that for some time now. "What is it she thinks I'll do for her?"

"She won't tell anyone but you. She said that it's personal. And because of that, she will not answer any of the questions put to her so that we may proceed with this pretrial." Raven glanced at her mother, then back at the judge again. "I'm begging you, Raven, to do this for us, please. I have a lot to get through today. I don't want to burden you, but I've seen you in action with her, and I think it would maybe set her up nicely if you were to tell her what you wish."

"Will you record it?" He said if she did this, he'd use his own phone to do that. "All right. But this will not be pretty, sir. I'm telling you right now that I don't like her, and I certainly will not be putting up with her shit."

"Good for you."

Raven walked to her mother just as one of the bailiffs walked to stand by her. He was holding a small device pointed at her mother, and she smiled at her. This was going to be ugly, Raven knew it.

"What is it you think you want me to do for you? I want you to think very hard on it, and realize that I'm going to tell you no." Merriam told her to keep her voice down. "I will not. You only lower yours when you think it suits whatever it is you're doing. Otherwise, you shout to the world what you're talking about. What is it?"

"I was told that you are pressing charges against me for trying to take that bastard child from you. Raven, she cannot be an Addington. Don't you get that? She's nothing. Not to me. She shouldn't be to you either. Get rid of all that nasty weight." Raven started to walk away. "Wait. I want you to have your father stop this divorce. How can I hope to become the next president of the club if I have a divorce hanging over my head? You tell him that I'm going to teach him a lesson if he doesn't take care of this right now. I'm an Addington, for Christ's sake, and we do not divorce."

"Apparently, having several dozen abortions is all right, though." Mother looked around and told her to keep her voice down again. No one needed to know that in here. "Ah, but they do know that. Everyone does. It's been in the newspaper, and I want you to know that I helped you out with that."

"It's about time that you did something by me. I've never done a thing to you that you didn't deserve. When are you going to get away from that man you supposedly married?" Raven said that they were still married and were going to have a child. "No. No, you can't do this to me. I demand that you abort it right now."

"Here? In this courtroom, right here on the floor? Why Mother, what would people say if I just popped out my child right here?" Mother called her all kinds of names then. Some of them Raven was sure that she was making up. When she called her a slut for what seemed like the millionth time since she'd found out she was having Molly, Raven had enough. "Watch your mouth, Mother. You want something from me, while I want nothing more to do with you."

"You have never been a good child to me, Raven. Never. Not since you were old enough to use that smart mouth of yours." Raven thanked her. "That is not something you should be proud of, Raven. I swear to you, you are the cruelest and most rotten person there is. I am still your mother, damn it. You contact your father, and you tell him that I want out of here. I do not belong here, and I will not tolerate him leaving me here as if I mean nothing to him and the name Addington."

"You don't, as a matter of fact. Besides, I don't know what has you so hyped up about getting home. The house has been sold. Daddy is living with my husband, daughter, and I while he thinks about what he wants to do from now on. One of my wonderful brothers-in-law is going to move in after everything in the place that you breathed on is stripped out. That's everything in the event you didn't know." Mother stood up and slammed her chained hands against the table. "What? Are you upset about something?"

"You tell him I will not allow that. I am going to live there even if I have to kill a lot of people to make it happen. You tell your father that it will be entirely his fault because he drove me to it." Raven reminded her mother that she was being recorded. She turned to look at the recorder before continuing. "Roger Addington, you will be at that house when I get out of here, or so help me, I will destroy you, both physically and financially, before your next heartbeat."

"Oh, before I forget to tell you. While we're on the subject of Dad, he's made it so that you're not an Addington. He's stripped you of that name because you were never the name that you changed it from when you married him. Also, and this is really funny to me—you signed a prenup. You're getting nothing. Not one red cent from Daddy, his estate, or me. Ever."

This time Raven did walk away from her. Mother was still screaming at her to get back to where she was. Raven, ignoring all the insults and nasty things she was being called, barely made it to the bathroom before she threw up. While she knew that it was never going to get better between them, she could be happy that her mother was going to be far away when this was finished. She wanted her not only in prison but in one that was far, far away from her. While in prison, she'd not be able to make calls every day. Mother would be unable to have people message Raven through the courts. It would be better for all of them when she was gone. Prison might even make her a better person. Raven wondered why she'd even bothered to come here today.

Hello, my darling. I can feel you're stressed out again. Should I come there as my cat and rescue you? Sawyer had a way about him that made her feel better with just a simple sentence. *I take it that nothing is going as planned at the courthouse today.*

Nothing. Worse than that, Mother is holding up the proceedings so that she can yell at me about the divorce and how I've ruined the good name of Addington. I shouldn't have come here. You were right. Sawyer said that he wasn't so sure that he had been. *What do you mean? You think I should have come here and been treated this way? Wow, that's harsh.*

No, I didn't mean that. I meant that – well, you have to admit, you were feeling a little doubtful about your mother and whether what she'd been doing was enough to warrant her being in prison. Did this help? She said that it had solidified it very well that she needed to be put away. *That's as good as any reason to be there, to figure this out on your own. You might have believed me a little that this was going to happen when we spoke about it. But you got to know first-hand that she's a fucking bitch who isn't going to change. Did you tell her about the house?*

I did. I'm so glad that Gunner is buying it from Dad. To be honest with you, every time I think about him living in that huge house, all I can think about is he'll be sleeping out on the back lawn in a sleeping bag rather than buying himself some nice furniture for it. Sawyer told her that Gunner was actually working with the people in the house. *Well, that's good, I guess. How is he handling being around people?*

I didn't say he was there when they were. He comes in after they're gone, and I guess one of them leaves him a list of stuff that he can do. Gunner told me that he's enjoying getting his hands dirty in a way that doesn't involve blood. Freaked me out a little when he said that. Raven laughed and got up from the floor to clean herself up. *There was another reason that I contacted you. How would you like to meet myself and Molly for dinner? I'll bring your grandma too. We could try out that restaurant that you were reading about, and then get Holly a car. She's been bugging me to do that for her.*

She said that she loves bugging you, so don't think this will be the end of her bothering you about things. She loves you. Sawyer told her that he loved her as well. *I'm going to go back to the hotel and take a short nap. Molly is at the packhouse, learning how to use the magic that she got from you. I still can't believe that she has so much from a few drops of your blood.*

I'm just glad that it's not much more than she has now. Being able to search out things that she wants and to bring them to her is nothing that I know how to do. I think she's a little upset that she can't shift. She was, Raven told him. *Okay – date or not?*

Yes. I'll take a nap at the hotel that I'm in, and you guys can meet me there. I do understand that they had to move the trial to a different place, but Columbus isn't that far away, do you think? He told her how it had a lot more people to choose from for jurors than their town. *I suppose. Okay, I'm better now. I'll go there and see you guys later. I can't wait for this to be done. Is Daddy all right?*

He is. I think that he's having a good time with my dad. They're working on the rose garden. Dad and he are learning how to drive the tractor and use the attachments. I guess Roger wants to put in a little garden someplace on the land that we have. I told him that would be fine by me. Mom is going to help him with it. She asked him about the peas. *Yes, the ground is plowed up, and the rows are set up and ready. Mom is so excited about having peas that she can't hardly stand it. Seems like a great deal of work for so little return, but then Mom will make it work to where she'll have bushels of them if I don't miss my bet.*

They were still laughing when she exited the bathroom. There were police all around this floor she was on. When one of them spotted her, Raven was escorted to the limo that was out front for her, and he made sure that she was in the hotel before he left. Whatever happened, because Sawyer said he'd not called anyone to escort her, Raven was glad they were taking care of her. Raven had a feeling that it had to do with her mother.

Exhaustion rolled over her in waves as soon as she got off the elevator on her floor. Even before she was able to get the covers pulled back on the bed, she was falling into it and closing her eyes. The baby and the stress were making it difficult for her to function. Raven decided that for her own peace of mind and health, she wasn't going back to the courthouse.

Chapter 2

Chandler wanted to meet the woman named Sasha. However, he wanted to do it on his own terms. He wasn't opposed to giving her a ride when she needed one. What he didn't like was that he felt like he was being set up by his own mother.

Did she really think that he was the best one for the job when his dad and Roger were using the fun equipment? He wanted to play in the dirt too. Chandler wanted to be a veterinarian in the worse sort of way, but there was nothing better, he thought than putting something in the ground and watching it mature and bear fruit. In this case, roses, but it was something that he loved doing too.

Knocking on the door, he was surprised to hear something like a squeak on the other side. Leaning into the door, laying his ear right against it, he tried the handle to the door and found it locked. That was when he heard someone calling for help.

Taking a couple of steps back from the door, he slammed his foot into the middle of the door, using a bit of his cat so he'd not hurt so badly afterward, and knocked the door in. The room looked as if it had been ransacked, but he was more concerned with the voices he heard in the next room.

Going into what turned out to be the bedroom, he found a man standing over a woman. He had a wooden bat in his hands, something that Chandler noticed was covered in blood. As the man started screaming at the woman on the bed to tell him—nothing else, but to tell him something—Chandler put his fingers in his mouth and whistled. He really had thought about just grabbing the bat but was afraid that he could have had a gun or a knife to finish the job he seemed intent on doing. Whistling, Chandler thought, would make him turn toward him, so he'd get to check him out and then kill him.

The man did turn, but then he disappeared. The bat dropped to the floor as if the man, who he knew had been holding it, hadn't been able to disappear with it. Chandler's first thought was vampire. But then why not take the bat? That was when he remembered the woman.

"Miss, are you all right?" She moaned, and Chandler

was careful when he rolled her to her back so that he could see her. "You're pretty beat to shit, ma'am. I'm sorry, but I think you might need some stitches. Did you piss off a vampire?"

"No. A dead man." Since he didn't know her or understand what she was talking about, he told her that he was going to the bathroom to get her a wet cloth. "There's a big first aid kit under the sink. Could you bring that to me?"

Opening up the cabinet, he pulled out the biggest first aid kit he'd ever seen. Taking it back to the bedroom, Chandler saw that she was sitting up, but she didn't look any better to him. Since he'd gotten the washcloth too, he began wiping at her face.

"What the hell are you doing? That hurts." He told her that he was sorry. "Holy fucking shit. What did you do to the door? Did you use a battering ram or something?"

"No. My foot. You're very snarky, aren't you? I came in here to save you." She looked around her bedroom and then at him. "Okay, I arrived much too late to actually save you, but he did leave when I got here."

"He caught me off guard, that— Did you say that you saw him? I mean, you said that he disappeared, so I'm assuming that you saw him." Chandler told her that he'd seen a man standing over her with a wooden bat. Then he pointed to the one on the floor. "He disappeared. You saw him. That's not right."

"Okay. Did he hit you pretty hard on the head?" She glared, and Chandler found himself wanting to burst out laughing. However, he had a feeling that she'd not find him all that funny right now. "Was it a vampire that hurt you? I mean, I know a couple of them. It could be that they might know who he was. I can—"

"He was dead." Chandler nodded. "Look, buster. I see the fucking dead. They've given me this fucking promotion, and now I not only see them, but they can touch me too. With ball bats. You sitting here humoring me is not helping me one bit. Why did you see him? For that matter, who the fuck are you?"

"Chandler Bishop. My mom sent me here so that I could take you to our home. I guess you're having dinner with us or something. But first I need to take you to the—" A woman entered the room, and Chandler asked her if she'd help him. "Miss Sasha is hurt, and I need to get her to the emergency room. Perhaps you know the guy that was here hurting her."

"You see her?" Chandler was getting a little frustrated by being asked if he saw all these people coming in and out of her room. "And damn it, your first name starts with a C. Are you him? The one that is going to come after me? I'll tell you right now, I'm not going to go easy. Where is the baby? Have you hurt her yet?"

"Hold on. Just hold on a minute. What baby? Pip? She's fine. Better than when I found her. Was that the man—? No, it couldn't have been, or you would have said so. Why ask me if I was the man if you thought it was the other guy? You're very confusing." She growled at him. "Lady, you have no idea how sexy that sounds to me. So, how about I get you patched up enough to go and see to your cuts, then we head to my parents' home? My brother Quincey will be there too, so he can make sure that you're doing all right."

Sasha didn't speak to him for the rest of the time he was there. She did let him help her get her shoes on, as well as help her into his car. Since it wasn't that far from where he was taking her to be looked at, he reached out to Sawyer and let him know what was going on at the house Sasha had been living in.

Is she hurt badly, you think? He told him that he didn't think so and that she kept telling him about dead people and wondering why he could see them. *Do you?*

No. I saw what I think was a vampire because he disappeared not long after I got there. And a woman. I don't remember catching her name. But Sasha seemed blown away—or more pissed, I'm not sure yet—that I could see both of them. Why the hell is that a big deal if I see anyone or not? I mean, Christ, it was like she has a one track mind. I think she got her head hit pretty hard.

Chandler, she sees ghosts. And talks to them. If she's asking you about why you can see them too, she's being serious. Chandler was glad that he'd stopped the car in the parking space, or he didn't want to think what might well have happened. *You keep me informed about her ER visit, and I'll see what I can figure out at her place. If it was a ghost, we can only assume that she's helped someone, and that was what got him dead. It could be Bradley Riddle. The man killed his wife by drowning. He was killed today when the police tried to take him in for questioning. You might want to mention that to her, that Riddle is dead.*

I will. She mentioned that my name started with a C. What does that mean? He said that he didn't know. *I have a lot of unanswered questions here, along with a woman that can see ghosts.*

You might want to figure that out too, why you can see ghosts. Might be something there too. Sawyer asked if she was his mate.

Mate? You bring that up now? Damn it, Sawyer. Just because you're happily married with a kid on the way, doesn't mean that the entire world needs to follow suit. I don't even have a place to live except with our parents. Why the fuck would a mate come along now?

Sawyer was still laughing when he closed the connection. He was a fucking moron, that was what he was. When they took Sasha back to one of the rooms, he sat down in the waiting room to wait. Less than a minute later, he was brought to her, as she had asked for him. Chandler was just glad to have someplace to sit while he cleared up some things in his head. But the woman had more questions for him. Chandler had some of his own.

"I was told that I wasn't all that nice to you." He didn't agree or disagree with her. "Well, I'm sorry. I've had a lot of extra stress added to my plate today, and it's making me short with people. You're the second person to have called me snarky in the last few days. The other person was your brother. Him, I like."

"I do too. He's calm and level headed. Unlike some people, I know." She growled, and he growled right back at her. "Look. I was to bring you home for dinner. I heard you crying out, and I went into your home, intending to help you. The man that was standing over you with a bat disappeared, and yes, I saw him. The woman—I didn't catch her name. I saw her too." Hailey appeared in the room and smiled at them both.

"Her name is Hailey Riddle." Chandler told her about the man named Riddle and asked her if he could be the same family. "He's her husband. The man who killed her. If he's dead too, that explains why, if it was him, he was there to beat me to shit. Hailey, did you tell him who I was?"

"No. I only said that I was glad that he'd gotten his just rewards. I didn't say a word about you." Chandler looked at the woman, and she smiled at him again. "I think he should see the real me, don't you? I don't know that it would make him any more believing, but it might be a step in the right direction."

Before he could ask what was going on, the women, Hailey, shifted from a very beautiful woman to one that looked as if she'd spent a fair amount of time underwater—like days. Standing up, slightly freaked out, he thought about all the things that his mind had blanked out when he'd broken into Sasha's place. He looked at Sasha when Hailey went back to her pretty self.

"The man that was beating you up, he had three bullet holes in his back. They weren't bleeding that way, so he must have been shot in the front. He also had one in his forehead that took out the back of his head." Chandler sat down again, his head spinning. "He was dead. She's dead."

"I tried to tell you that. So now that you've figured it out, it must be true, correct?" He asked her who had hurt her in the past. "I don't know what you mean."

"Sure, you do. Someone out there—a male, I'm thinking—belittled you a great deal, thinking that you, as a woman, didn't have the smarts to work at whatever he was doing. I'm not him." She said that she knew that. "Do you? I don't think you do. I think—and this is probably just me—but I think you lump all men in the same category, and that is the end of it. As I said, I'm not him."

He stood up, and she looked panicky. His cat wanted to leap out and take care of whatever was going on. Then when she spoke, he looked around too. "Do you see them here? All of the people here in his part of the room with us?"

"Yes. So?" She told him that they were all dead. "No. That doesn't seem right. First of all, I've never seen the dead before. I'm not saying that you don't. My brother, he said you can talk to them as well. But I don't."

"You do now. I have a feeling that I know why, but you have to tell me for sure. Am I your mate, Chandler? I mean, I haven't any idea why I think that other than you've picked up the same traits that I have. So can you please tell me if I'm right?" He leaned into her neck and smelled the fresh blood. Licking the wound there so that he could get rid of the smells, the wound sealed. That alone should have confirmed what she was asking him, but he took a deep breath of her and staggered back from the scent. "I am, aren't I? I'm your mate, and now we can both see the dead."

"I don't know what's going on here." She assured him that she didn't either. "I didn't smell you before. I mean, at your house. You smelled of blood. I'm sorry. Just give me a minute to make this right. Not that I'm not happy—I'm just dealing with the whole dead thing right now."

"Go ahead and take your time. There are only about twenty ghosts here that need help." Snarky again, but he understood it now. "Do you need a nap too? Perhaps I can have them bring you in a bed to lie on. Also, I'm sure that with a hospital this large, they'd have you a binky should you need it."

"Look, you've had your entire life to deal with this. I've had ten minutes or less. Seeing the dead isn't something that I ever thought about before." When she started crying, he sat down on the bed with her. Pulling her into his arms, he finally pulled her onto his lap so that he could hold her better. "I'm so very sorry. I'm not mad at you—I'm not mad at anyone. But I am trying very hard to figure this out. I shouldn't have taken it out on you while I was doing so. I'm very sorry."

"It's fine. I hurt really badly, and I think I might have taken that out on you as well." He said it was understandable. "The nurse over there said that you're going to be asked to leave. Did you hear her?"

"No. I was groveling to you." He smiled, and the nurse was suddenly in front of him. She'd been hurt; it looked to him like she'd fallen down a flight or two of stairs. "I'm so sorry about your accident. I hope you didn't suffer badly."

"I didn't, young man. I tripped up on my own and would have lived except for the fact that I don't usually take the stairs, so they didn't know to look for me there. Trying to be healthy got me dead. But here is my advice to you both. Tell them that the two of you are married, or they'll kick you out of here. You look as if you need each other." Chandler said that he didn't want to leave Sasha like this, then asked the nurse what she needed from him. "Nothing. I like being here. I help the younger nurses out when they seem like they're struggling. Sometimes I even get the doctors to listen up. I'm all right here."

Nodding, Chandler wasn't sure what he would have done to help her anyway. But he did keep holding onto Sasha. When a nurse came in, the dead nurse told him that she was real. He'd have to figure that out soon enough, he supposed. They were taking Sasha to get x-rays.

"I'll be here when you get back." Just as he'd been told, they asked him what his relationship with Sasha was. "She's my wife. Someone broke into our home while I was out and beat her up. I've called the cops. My brother, Sawyer, is going to make sure that they find the bastard. My name is Chandler Bishop. My brother is married to Raven."

"I know her and your brother. I'm sorry, Mr. Bishop. You can never be too sure about people nowadays. You can wait right here. I will tell you that they'll more than likely admit her, just to make sure that her head wounds aren't that bad. But I'll fix it up so that you can stay with her." Chandler thanked the nurse. "I'll be right back with something for you to drink."

When he was alone, Chandler paced the small space. Not only did he have a mate now, but they shared the fact that they could see ghosts, something that he'd never thought he'd have to say. Chandler thought about letting his family know what was going on and that he had a mate, but decided that he needed more time to get used to the idea. A mate. Who helped ghosts. What is going to happen next? his mind screamed at him. The dead would rise up from the ground and kill them both.

~*~

Katie didn't know what to think about her daughter. It was bad enough that Sasha was a pain in the ass, but when Pearl started acting up too, she wanted to get up and knock some sense into their hard heads. Not that she could do any of that. Katie was stuck in a wheelchair for the rest of her life—or so everyone thought. Her kids were just stupid enough to believe everything she said. Or at least, the other two besides Sasha. Katie was sure that she knew something was up.

"Mom, have you seen my car keys? I left them by the front door." Katie told him that the last time she drove his car, she laid them right back so he'd not notice that she'd gone out. "Ha. That's funny. Because you can't drive. Much less walk. You're a riot, Mom. A real funny person."

She knew that he believed she was funny when all along, she was being sarcastic. And truthful too. Katie had borrowed his car and had put the keys back where she'd gotten them. She'd gone to see if her daughter was home, and why she wasn't picking up her phone when she called her. The keys were right there by the front door in the bowl that had been put there for that purpose. Her children were all morons.

"I found them." She didn't even bother telling him good job since he'd found them where he knew they were supposed to be. "I'll be late coming home tonight, Mom. Don't wait up for me. I'll see you sometime tomorrow afternoon."

When she heard the front door not just click closed, but also the lock engage, she stood up from her confinement, then stretched. Sometimes the kids would hang around for days before she'd be able to do this. Katie wondered what they'd say if they could see her right now. Probably get mad at her. They were ungrateful shits.

Dragging the chair with her, she walked to the bar in the living room. She wasn't going to be caught unawares again. Once when she'd been up and around, one of them came home and nearly caught her with the chair across the room from her. She'd had to tell them that she had fallen, then gotten pissy with them when they asked her about the chair. The only one that didn't believe her, and doubted the story of why she was where she had been, was Sasha. If she had been there when she'd been caught, Katie wouldn't have been able to milk the system anymore, nor would she have been able to get the special treatment that she had learned to love. Special parking for the car that was carting her around. Even the movie theaters gave special seating to people that had a wheelchair. There were all kinds of perks she'd gotten since she had had her accident.

Not *all* the doctors believed her when she told them that she couldn't walk. Those that didn't had called it psychosomatic, or something like that. They thought there wasn't anything wrong with her, and that she should easily be able to get up and walk around. She could, but not where anyone would see her.

The doctors that did believe that she was hurt and unable to do for herself made sure that she had the nicest wheelchair, as well as all kinds of medications that she'd been selling on the Internet since she no longer needed them for herself. It was a very profitable side business for her.

Katie looked at the envelope that she'd gotten today in the mail. She had been going out to get the mail since she'd taken to the chair, weeding out things that the kids didn't need to know about. Like her money, for one thing. The other was insurance shit, like the one she'd gotten today.

She had to go before a panel of doctors to determine if her doctor was doing enough for her. He was doing just fine, but they said in the letter that if she didn't comply they'd cut her off and make her return all the money that they'd shelled out for things like the drugs, her chair, as well as the nurse that came in once a week to get her legs into shape. Katie was nervous about this.

Sasha could call them. She'd done it before when Katie had told her that she'd been in too much pain to be traveling in a car. But since the time she'd nearly gotten caught walking, Sasha hadn't done anything for her. She wouldn't even allow her to bum a ride from her to the mall. Nothing.

Katie didn't know what was wrong with her daughter, but right now, she didn't have time to deal with her. The insurance company was saying that she had two days to prepare herself for the visit. They weren't going to allow her to even get out of the house for this—they were coming here to make sure their money was going to good use, she supposed. It was, Katie thought with a laugh, just not what they wanted it to go to.

Hearing the lock in the front door had her sitting down and covering her legs up again. Pretending to be reaching for something had Pearl scrambling to get to her before she tipped over. She shouted and pushed her away from the cabinet.

"Are you even supposed to be drinking while on some of those medications you're on?" Katie, acting as pitiful as she could, asked her why it mattered anymore. "Because I want you around, Mom. Not attached to a breathing machine, that is the only thing keeping you alive. You can have a little but not a full glass of it. Okay?"

"I am a grown woman, Pearl. I know my limits." Pearl changed the subject, which Katie only just realized she was very good at and told her about the dress she'd gotten on sale today. "A dress? Do you have any idea how long it's been since I've been in a dress and heels?"

Last night, she told herself, and she had looked damned good in them too. But Pearl was going on about a wedding that she'd been invited to, and how she wanted to show off all the weight she'd lost. Katie never saw evidence of this supposed weight that she'd shed, but she kept insisting that it was falling off her in buckets.

Looking at the tags that claimed the size of the dress, Katie wondered how on earth her heavy daughter was going to squeeze her body into a size four. Twenty-four, maybe, but a four? There wasn't any way that she'd be able to get the sucker up over one leg. Opening her mouth to tell her that she noticed that Pearl was reading the letter from the insurance company.

"When did this arrive? What do they mean that there is some suspicion about your claims? Mom, what's going on?" Katie told her that the neighbor boy had brought the letter to her, as it had been put in the wrong box. "Okay, that makes sense. But why are they saying these things about you? About how they want a panel of their doctors to see you? Did you call them to ask what's going on?"

"I've not had an opportunity to yet. He only just brought it over a little while ago. You might have even passed him on his way back home." She said that she hadn't seen anyone. "I don't know what to think about all this. That's why I wanted a drink before I give them a call. Give it back to me, Pearl, and I'll call them in the morning."

"I'll do it." Well, hell, that wouldn't work, now would it? She told Pearl that she wanted to do it. "I'll call them. And I'll give them a piece of my mind while I'm at it, too. To send you something like this, accusing you of faking shit when you're stuck here all day. I'll call them and—"

"Damn it, Pearl, give me the fucking letter." She snatched it out of her hand when she was close enough to do so. Calming herself now that she had the numbers back so that Pearl wouldn't be able to call, she looked at her. "I don't get to do a great deal around here anymore. I mean, you guys get to go to work and out to weddings while I'm stuck here. The least I can do, that I want to do, is to call about my own health. I'm sorry that I yelled at you. But as you can imagine, I get all worked up and worry that they'll tell someone that I'm fine, and then where will I be without all the meds and this chair?"

"I'm sorry, Mom." She took the hug when it was offered to her. When Pearl stood up, she said she'd order them some dinner. "That way we'll have more time to watch that show we've been watching together. All right?"

"Yes, that would be wonderful. I don't suppose you've heard from Sasha, have you? I mean, she used to send me money all the time, remember? That sure was helpful in purchasing my meds, you know. But it seems like here lately, there hasn't been anything in the mail from her." Pearl asked if she could call her for her. "I'd like that. She and you, you used to be close, didn't you?"

"Not for a very long time. Sasha doesn't have a great deal to do with many people, I guess. And I haven't seen her name in the paper since she was accused of being a fraud. I knew that was going to catch up with her someday. Claiming to see the dead. Can you believe that?" Katie did believe it because that was one of the reasons that Sasha had moved out. Because someone dead had ratted Katie out about the drugs and shit that she was selling. That was another thing that had pissed Katie off. That people could tell on her about shit she'd sold to them that wasn't up to par. "I'll call her right after I make the call to get some pizza. Remind me to only have a couple of slices, Mom. I need to keep this weight from coming back."

Katie nearly laughed when she heard Pearl order three extra-large pizzas with extra meat and cheese. Pearl knew that her brother had gone out. So who did she think was going to be eating all that pizza? She would, Katie knew it. Pearl could devour a large pizza in ten minutes.

She was still on the phone with her sister, or someone, when the delivery guy came. Handing him the money, she noticed that Pearl was giving him a twenty dollar tip. Before she could change that out for something smaller, like a buck, the kid had snatched it from Pearl and took off running. Fucker. That money would have gotten her some nice drugs for herself. The ones that she sold were no longer working to give her the high that she wanted. And Katie did like a little buzz for herself once in a while.

While they ate their meal, Katie only having about half of one of the pizzas and Pearl working on the third one, they watched their show. Something was forever hunting someone or killing them. Katie only half paid attention to the shit going on. She mostly watched it for ideas. Like how to scam people.

Of course, tonight, there was nothing about how to get out of a panel of doctors coming to see you. She needed to get this shit figured out before they arrived, or she really was going to be in a wheelchair. Her kids would make sure of it after all they'd done for her.

"I left three messages with Sasha, Mom. She's not called me back yet. I'll make sure that my phone is close by me when I go up to bed. That way, if she does get around to calling, I can hear it." Katie asked her where she was. "She's not at her apartment? Gee, Mom, I don't know if she's not there. How did you know about her not being home?"

"I think your brother told me. Zack went to see her and said the place was empty." She'd have to remember to tell Zach that Pearl told her that Sasha wasn't home. That way, she'd not get her story too messed up. "When you talk to her, ask her please to come and talk to me. I miss her. Even though she is a crackpot, I miss her."

Yeah, Katie thought, like she missed having her ex-husband around. He was as dull as her daughter was, forever going on about ghosts and the dead. Shivering when it felt like something touched her, Katie looked around. Getting spooked about supposed ghosts did that to her sometimes.

Chapter 3

Chandler could feel her anxiety now. He thought about finding out what was going on but remembered that he'd taken her blood so he should be able to contact her that way. Gently touching her mind with his, he was glad that she didn't yell at him when he asked her if she was all right.

They tell you to relax and not to move while you're in one of these things. Then the noise is so loud that it hurts my ears. Also, the moment someone tells you not to move, your nose itches or your fingers want to twitch. There is also a ghost in here that is making weird faces at me. He told her that they could talk about something if that would help. *Like what? You telling me that you can't see ghosts? Or would you like to go down the route of you seeing them as well as I do?*

How about just a tit for tat about each other? I'm going

to college to become a veterinarian. That's been my dream since I was a child. She said that she'd wanted to take pictures—of wildlife. *That sounds wonderful. To be out in the wild and being able to bring back memories as well as making them for others.*

Do you always see the bright side of something? He said that he did try to. *I've not seen the bright side of anything since I figured out why there were people hanging around me all the time. As a kid, you barely understand death. Having them come to you when they're straight from the accident isn't all that much fun.*

I'm sorry. Perhaps I can give you a hand with this, and it won't be so tough on you. She said that would be good. *I have five brothers, my parents, as well as my sister-in-law, Raven, and her family. It's just her dad, Roger, and grandma, Holly, who we all love, but she's wonderful. Also, Raven has a daughter named Molly, who has charmed her way into our hearts. Molly is nine.*

He did wonder if he should mention that Raven's mother was going to prison, but he didn't want to scare Sasha off too soon. She laughed and told him that the ghost that was making faces at her had died a long time ago, and he had wanted to be a clown.

He makes people try and forget what they're here for. I told him that I had you, and he's gone now. I was afraid that I'd made him upset, but he said that he was headed to the children's ward and would be back later. Such a nice thing for him to do. She let out a long sigh before speaking again. *I have a brother, Zack, and a sister, Pearl. They both live with my mom because she claims that she's handicapped, confined to a wheelchair. She's not. In fact, I would say that she's probably healthier than Pearl is. Last time I saw her, she was carrying a lot of extra weight. They both work, which is good, but Mom is pulling them down with what she's doing while they're gone.*

What is it she's doing that is going to hurt them? Sasha told him that her mom was selling off the drugs that she got and pocketing the money. *That's not good. I mean, if she's mailing the stuff out, not only can they get her for drugs and paraphernalia, but also mail fraud. I'm not sure what it's called, but my brother Sawyer would know.*

I don't have any money. I can't hold down a proper job because of the visitors that come to me at all hours. The last of my money was used to come here in search of Hailey. He told her that Raven had money, and she was helping them all out so that they could finish up college. *That's very kind of her. I don't know her, but I did know her dad. Roger Addington is a very nice man. His wife, she could go fuck herself for all I care.*

She's going to prison. Sasha said that was a good place for her. *Yes, that's what we all think. Recently she kidnapped Molly and hurt her badly. If not for Sawyer helping her along with his blood, she might well have died. As it is, Merriam is going to be gone for a very long time for all kinds of things. Including murder.*

If Raven needs help in finding the dead, I can help her with that. In fact, I'd very much love to help her. Chandler asked Sasha what had happened between Merriam and herself. *I used to work at the club that she belonged to. Merriam made this huge fuss about the flowers on the table, and I only said that I thought they were very pretty, but I'd move them. Apparently, that's an ongoing thing for her, to complain about something then be the martyr when it comes to leaving things the way they were. I simply removed the flowers, and therefore gave her reason to complain. She wanted me flogged – I kid you not, flogged – for making the flower arrangement make her sneeze. I wasn't really fired, but they did tell me not to come back when she was there. So I just didn't return.*

I would imagine it would be hard to hold down a job when you see the dead all around you. She said that he'd get used to it. *There are three in the room with me now. The nurse, who is Ruby, by the way, is showing me how to tell the difference between the living and the dead. It's getting easier. Ruby said that the dead can't speak to each other unless they died at the same time. Is that right?*

Yes. And it's weird about that. They don't have to be in the same area as long as they died at the same time. Like, I had two people that didn't know each other, but since their deaths occurred at the same time, thousands of miles apart, they could have spoken to each other. However, the language barrier didn't help. That's another thing you'll figure out. It doesn't matter what language they speak, you'll hear English from them. Makes it nicer for you to get to the bottom of things faster. Chandler said that would make things easier for him for sure. *I didn't realize that I could understand what they were saying until someone pointed it out to me. I think it was in the paper that a person that I'd helped had only spoken French. I can't speak that. I'm on my way back to you. I don't know what they found on the x-ray, but another man came in to talk to them before they would allow me to be released. Are you all right?* He told her that they were moving him to her room. *So, no home cooked meal for me tonight.*

She laughed, but he could tell that she was nervous. *How about after we find out your restrictions – if there are any – I can go out and get us something to eat, and we can share it in your room?* Sasha told him that would be wonderful. *Great. I can and will eat just about anything. You tell me what you want, and I'll make it happen. Also, what do you want to drink?*

I would love a pizza with everything – yes, all of it – all over it. I'm a meat eater too. He said that he knew just the place to get it from. *If you say Harvey's, I'm going to be in love with you right this minute.*

Sasha entered the room with him laughing. Apparently, they had the same taste in pizza places. When she was settled into her room, Chandler stepped out to give her a moment to change. He reached out to everyone to let them know what he had done.

And she's my mate. We figured that out...well, she figured it out before I did. Once I go and get us something to eat and bring it back, I'm going to stay here with her. The staff thinks that we're married so that I can stay with her, or they'd kick me out. Mom was so excited that she told him several times that she loved him. *I love you as well. All of you.*

Do you know anything about her being beaten up? I checked out her room, and whoever was there had torn it to shreds before he found her, I think. There isn't any blood in the living area at all. Chandler told Sawyer that he'd check with her when she was finished up with the nurses. *Chandler, I don't have to tell you that what she can do will be dangerous to her. And now to you too.*

I know. That's one of the main reasons that I'm staying here. By the way, Raven, she told me that she could help you with any bodies that you're looking for. She knows a great deal about your mother. Raven told him that she'd take her up on that. *Good. I'll let her know. We're just getting to know each other, as I said. Right now, we're just waiting on the doctor to come by and tell her what her CT scan said. Sasha thinks there might have been some concern over it when they were doing it. How's Pip doing? I never thought that I'd say this, but I miss the little girl.*

She's doing well. Molly is having a grand time with

her, feeding her, and even changing her diaper. I think she's getting into practice for when her brother or sister comes along. Chandler could hear the happiness in his brother's voice when he talked about his children. *Mom and Dad are going to act as a holding place for her until they find someone that can come to pick her up. We know nothing about the woman that had her other than her name was Melinda.*

I'll talk to Sasha about her. Maybe something else has come up, and she might know more. I didn't want to bring it all up while she was getting her scan finished up. Raven said that was probably a good idea. *I have them on occasion.*

You do all the time. His dad and his protector jumped to his defense. *We have your mom's gardens all done up and ready. That new tractor of Wesley's sure did make short work of the job. We might have gone a little over the top, but I'm sure your mom can find something to put in the ground.*

When he closed the connection, Chandler stood in the hall for a few minutes more. The staff had come out and told him that he could go in now, but he waited. They might think that Sasha was ready for him to come in, but he didn't know if he was. This was a big step he was taking—both of them were taking.

"Hey." She was sitting in the middle of the bed, crying when he finally got the nerve to go see her. "What's wrong? Did one of those nurses hurt you? Say something to you?"

"I thought you'd left me here." He held her after sitting on the bed until she seemed to gather herself up. "I have something that I need to tell you. I didn't tell anyone yet because I was still trying to deal with things that had been said to me. The woman from today, she's my sister. One that I didn't know I had. Melinda Harvard is her name."

"Sawyer wanted me to talk to you to see if something had come to you about her. Why didn't you tell him? Was it because you wanted to see if she was telling you the truth or not? I can understand that." Sasha told him it was because she was terrified. Then she told him about the baby. "Pip is yours to raise? That's wonderful. I mean, if you want to raise her. She's already a huge hit at my parents' home."

"Do you know if she has a mark on the bottom of her left foot?" Since he knew for sure that she did, he told her that. "I do as well. Melinda said that she'd be like me. Have the ability to help the ghosts when she was old enough to do so."

"So, you didn't get hurt to become what you are." Sasha said that she'd been hurt in the womb before she was born. "Sort of a trauma? Pip had that as well. Being born the way she was, cut from the womb like that, I'm sure that she would be considered having trauma as well. What do you want to do about her? This is something that you have to decide on, Sasha. I'm all for raising her as my own, but she's related to you."

"I didn't think I wanted anything to do with her, only because I don't have a stable home—no home at all. No money. No job. I have nothing at all to offer her. I'm not even sure that I'd be able to take her if the state or someone else is involved in making that decision." He said that he could get them a place to live. And he would find a job. "What about your education? I don't want you to give that up, Chandler. That would be so unfair."

"So would leaving Pip to the system. I'm sure they have lots of nice people that would do a great job with raising her, but I have a feeling that she's going to need special care. Not to mention learning how to use her craft. I believe that you're the only one that can teach that properly. Don't you?" Sasha nodded. "Then it's settled. I'll find us a place to live, close to my family for support, and then get a job. This is my dream now, and I couldn't be happier."

He was happy too. He had a mate; Chandler had a little girl. Things could not have been better. Now all he had to do was to pay back the loan from Raven about classes and see if he could keep the car that Sawyer had given him. Also, find them a house and furnish it. Sure, he thought, piece of cake.

~*~

Raven didn't know what to do now. She's just

spoken to Chandler for the last two hours about things that he needed to take care of his new little family. Thinking of how hard it had been on her and Molly when she'd started out made her think that Chandler was going to make it happen no matter what she thought might go wrong. And so much could go wrong with something like this. What most concerned her was the fact that they both would have to show the courts that with them was going to be the best place for Pip to be raised. With what Chandler had just told her, Raven didn't think either of them had a snowball's chance in hell of making that happen.

"What's up?" She smiled at Sawyer when he joined her in the office. "You looked distressed. What did the doctor tell you about dealing with the little things? You need to also have your feet up."

"You're the one that is forever making me put my feet up. He only said that it's a good idea when I'm in the last trimester. Not every minute of every day." Sawyer started to massage her feet. "I need to talk something over with you. But I don't want you to jump in and take it over. Okay?"

"I don't do that." She just stared at him. "All right, I do that. But only if I can see that they need it. You said to me yourself, 'What's the point of having money if you can't help others?' So who is it we're going to be helping?"

"Chandler." Sawyer didn't say anything, but he did start massaging her feet harder. "He's not going to college. Did you know that?"

"He told Mom and Dad that he had more important things to take care of first. He didn't tell us or me what that might be." Raven pulled her feet from Sawyer before he made mush of them. "You've spoken to him, haven't you?"

"Yes. He's going to find him and Sasha a cheap rental so that they can be a stable home for Pip. Pip is her niece." Sawyer hadn't known that Raven could tell. "Then he's going to find him a job so that Sasha can continue to do what she does best—his words—and help the dead. While I love the idea of him giving up everything for his new family, I hate it too. I don't want him to give up his dreams for this."

"He won't see it as giving up anything, Raven. He'll just tell you that his priorities have changed." Raven told him that was exactly what he'd said to her. "You want to pave the way for him, don't you?"

"No. I want to do it all for him. Get him a lovely home, a good job doing what he loves best, and hire them a staff so that Pip is safe all the time." Sawyer asked her why she'd not be safe with them. "She would be safe, more than most kids like her. And by like her, I mean she's just like Sasha. When she gets a little older, she'll be helping the dead as well."

"I see." He seemed to have gotten something when he looked at her. "The man that killed her mom, he did that so that he could get rid of someone talking to the dead and telling on him."

"Sort of. He thought that he was killing Sasha and the child that she carried." Sawyer got up to pace. Watching him do that, she was glad that he was no longer touching her feet. He'd have broken them. "Chandler is going to ask for help from us all, but not in the way that I'd like to help him. He wants us to help him make sure that his mate and child are safe if anything happens to him when he figures out who this man is."

"He needs to move in here with us so that he can be safe." Raven told him that he wouldn't do that. "Why not? Is he too good to live in a really nice house with people just begging for him to let them help?"

"No. And get your head out of your ass. When did he ever act like that? He won't stay here because I have my dad, your parents come and go all the time, as well as the staff. He doesn't want anything to happen to any of those people, which includes our unborn child and Molly, because the man seems to not stop at such things as murder and the killing of unborn children. He's done it once. Chandler doesn't want it to happen again."

"Oh." She wanted to smack him and to hug him

too. "What are we going to do then? I can't just stand by and let him struggle with any of this. I'm sure that you have a plan all laid out, and know where he's going to be living. I do hope that it's close by. I love seeing all my family."

"It's close, but he's not going to like it." Sawyer said that was just tough. "Yes, I had hoped you'd say that. I just have to talk to your parents and my grandma to get him moving in the right direction. I'm sure that those three alone will have him making better choices."

"They're going to bully him, aren't they?" Raven laughed when Sawyer rubbed his hands together like he was in charge of the entire plan. "I want to bully him too. I don't think I want to mess with Sasha. She's a great deal like you, and she might well hurt me."

"Oh, I'm sure you're right on that score. Just hearing about her, I already love her to pieces. But we have to move on this in a way that doesn't make them hate us. I don't believe Chandler could ever hate his family, but we don't know Sasha that well. And since she is the one that Chandler will want to please in every way, we have to make this move in her direction in a sort of gentle bullying way." He asked her if that was really something. "I don't know. I'm making this up as I go. I do hope that your parents will know what to do. None of us have really met her except Chandler, so we have to take it from there."

When Sawyer left her, Raven looked at the house that she was hoping to get Chandler to move into. Picking up the other three pictures of homes that she'd purchased, she wondered what the other brothers would say when she told them that she'd gotten them houses too. Thinking on that, she wondered if she could make that work. It was a, "Here, I got you a house the same as I did the others, and this is where you're going to live," sort of thing. It was worth a shot. But first, she was going to talk to Saul and Sippy. And her daughter. Molly might just be the ticket for all of them.

Grinning, she picked up her phone. Calling her daughter to come home for a little while, that she had a project for her, had Molly giddy. Raven loved her daughter and the way that she'd been so accepting of all the things going on around them.

However, she had noticed that Molly never mentioned or joined in conversations about Raven's mom. Merriam, after the kidnapping, had become nothing to her. Which, Raven supposed, was a good thing. Her mother had wanted Molly dead even before she'd been born.

Half an hour later, Molly was home, and so was her grandma. They both were excited to be a part of this. Grandma was mad, just a little, that she'd not thought of it. Raven was glad that they were on board more than that she was appeasing her grandma. This had to be done in a way that she didn't turn out to be a snobbish bitch that was bringing everyone up to her and Sawyer's level. Really, all Raven wanted was for every one of them to be as happy as she was.

"I'm going to work on Uncle Chandler. I spoke to him yesterday, and he was stressed out." Raven asked Molly if he'd told her why. "No. He just said that he'd get it worked out. He also told me that he and Sasha are going to raise Pip. He sounded nervous about that as well."

"Pip? Why? You did ask him why, didn't you, love?" Raven was glad that Grandma had asked because she wanted to know as well. Molly told them what she'd found out. "The mother of that child was her sister? Oh my, that must have been very difficult for her. To see her sister like that."

"I don't think they knew each other."

Molly flounced away, something that Raven had only just noticed her doing. Looking at her grandma, Raven asked her how that was even possible.

"I don't know, to be honest. This gets stranger and stranger daily, don't you think?" Raven told her that she didn't know what to think. "Me either, if you want the truth of it. But I do know one thing. It will turn out well for them and the rest of us. Of that, I can always be sure with this family."

Raven hoped so. This was going to be a true test

of them trusting her again, she thought. She'd not just helped Chandler along, but the rest of them as well. Since Gunner had only paid her dad a quarter for his home, she thought that it was working out very nicely. If they would let her do this.

Chapter 4

Merriam tapped her foot when the second hand went past the twelve again. Where was he? She had given specific instructions on not just what she wanted to speak to Roger about, but also what she wanted him to do for her. These people in here were not treating her like she was an Addington, and she wanted them fired from their jobs. Also, he'd better be working on getting her home—to her home—so that she could take care of this nonsense of him thinking that he had her permission to divorce her and sell the house.

"Moron." She looked around to make sure that no one heard her. Addingtons didn't call people names when they were out in public. Unless, of course, she wanted the world to know what sort of idiots she had to work with. Roger had better get his act together, or she was going to come down on him like a load of bricks. She might just have to beat him with one of them. Merriam wasn't opposed to having him killed, or even killing him herself. Things were not pleasing to her.

When her mother-in-law sat across from her, Merriam ignored her. It was difficult to do at the best of times. With her just going on and on about things right now, in that loud, I-don't-care-who-hears-me voice, it was harder. Finally, having had enough, she turned to her.

"Will you please shut the fuck up? I have no reason to be speaking to you, and I find that I don't want you coming around at all. Now, where is Roger? He was supposed to be here five minutes ago." Holly said that he wasn't coming. "Of course, he is. I demanded for him to show up, and he had damn well better start listening to me."

"I don't think he cares one way or the other if you ever see him again, Merriam. I do, however, come bearing gifts. None that I think you're going to care about, but I have them all the same. Look. I have an ultrasound picture of the newest grandbaby." Merriam didn't even bother looking at the small black and white photo. "I have several copies, just in case you were to have a pissy fit and tear it up. The doctor said that both mom and baby are doing very well. He did tell her that it was going to be a big baby. Not like you think it is big at eight pounds, but more like eleven or twelve pounds. Like a small turkey."

"Why do you think that I'd care about my stupid daughter breeding another child? I suppose I should be thankful that she's married this time. But it won't last. He'll leave her as soon as I'm out of here." Holly asked her why she thought she'd be getting out of jail. "I'm an Addington. People such as I do not go to jail like a commoner. I swear to you, Holly, you are the dumbest person alive who has money. I should make sure to add that to my list of things to do when I'm out of here. To put you in a nursing home so that you'll not be out spending your money like you've only just found out you have it."

"I think I've done all right with managing my money, Merriam. I did tell Roger to make sure you signed a prenup so that you'd not try to take him to the cleaners when he finally got some sense in his head about you. You always were too uppity for me." Holly laughed. "I don't even know where you got the stick up your ass. You came from nothing at all. Not to mention, you murdered your entire family for no other reason than you could. We're finding out a lot about you as a child, did you know that? For instance, your sister said that you were nothing more than an easy person. I don't think she meant that in the nicest way. She was referring to how many of the town's men and boys you 'entertained.' It seems you weren't all that picky about getting a little something from them. Was it worth it?"

"I have no idea what you're talking about. And I would appreciate it if you kept your lies to yourself. I've no time for your stupidity today. Where is Roger?" She told her again that he wasn't coming. "He told you that, but I know him much better than you ever will, Holly. He was my husband for nearly thirty years."

"Yes, well, he has been my son for his entire life. I think that is longer than you knew him. However, I don't think you'd recognize him now. He's wearing jeans and T-shirts. You should see him in the yard playing with Molly. They have such a good time. Today they're going pumpkin hunting." Merriam looked at Holly, not believing the things that she was saying. "I have a picture of him. See?"

She took this picture. There wasn't any way that her husband, an Addington, would be wearing anything other than an impeccable suit and a silk tie. Holly told her that they were in the back yard of Sawyer's home. He was the man at the grill.

Merriam could only stare at the face of the man she'd been married to for so long. He looked twenty years younger—happy too. In fact, happier than she'd ever seen him. Merriam thought that he'd lost weight, and had a lovely glow to his face. Even with his hair all mussed up, she thought that he looked better than he ever had.

Handing the photo back to Holly, she turned her nose up to her. "He's too thin. And if he thinks I'm going to allow him to wear those sorts of things when I get out of here, he'd better be rethinking his lifestyle. I won't tolerate it." Holly only laughed as she put the picture away. "Why do you think my wanting to keep the Addington name pure is funny? My goodness, you'd think that you of all people would be thrilled someone is finally taking this name and making it more than just a laughingstock. Addington means something because of me."

"Yes, it does. Thanks to you, my husband's last name is now associated with a murderer, kidnapper, as well as a crazy fucking bitch that should never have been allowed out of her home to infect wonderful people like her daughter, her granddaughter, and the one on the way." Holly stood up, and Merriam just sat there. It wasn't that she didn't want to stand toe to toe to the old bitty, but she was chained to the floor. "I only came by to tell you that Roger, my son, is happier than he's ever been. No thanks to you. Also, Raven and Molly are nearly shining brighter than the sun because someone loves them. Again, no thanks to your interfering. I won't be back either. And you should simply give up on Roger coming here. He won't. Nor will Raven again. You've burned those bridges quite nicely."

"I didn't want to see you anyway. The sooner that you're gone, the better it will be for me. At least the people here know what my needs are and attend to every one of them." Holly just laughed like she'd just heard the funniest joke ever told. "Will you keep your voice down? You sound like a braying jackass when you laugh like that. Have you no shame?"

"I do. I'm ashamed that I ever called you my daughter-in-law. As for my laughter? I suppose you of all people know what a braying jackass sounds like. Your family had a couple of them, I'm to understand. You killed them, too, by setting fire to your family home. If I remember correctly, their names were Jack and Jill. Isn't that right?"

Holly knew entirely too much about her, and that pissed Merriam off. Where the hell was she getting this sort of information? All her family was dead, thanks to her. There had to be someone out there that was spouting off things they knew nothing at all about.

Merriam was taken back to her cell without seeing Roger. Tossing things around after the cop left her, she sat down on the mess she'd made.

There wasn't a single person catering to her every need. They barely acknowledged her at all unless she made a huge fuss about something. All that usually got her was the night guard coming by her cell every three minutes, it felt like, and banging on her bars until she was awake.

Merriam had to eat white bread with the rest of the people in here. Sandwiches with the crust still on them. Nasty meat sandwiches that didn't have any kind of garnish on the plate, unless she counted the bag of baked chips that she never ate.

Being treated like everyone else was something that she'd not experienced since she'd left home. Well, not right after leaving home. She'd had to lie, cheat, and steal her way into the position where she'd meet Roger. Christ, he'd been such easy prey for her. A man with money, and not a single prospect for a wife. At least there weren't any prospects for one after she put her claws into him. Not another woman around would dare go near him for fear of her. All it took was for her to mess up the faces of a couple of the women to make sure they understood that Merriam was going to get him. Once she did, she had him dangling at the end of her line, everything that she ever wanted fell right into her lap. But, she supposed, even that didn't go right.

He'd wanted children. Merriam told him that she wanted several too, but deep inside, she knew that she'd never have a child. Never allow one to stretch out her body and make her flabby. But no matter how much she'd tried to rid herself of Raven, the child just wouldn't let go. So, without her consent, not only did she have one, but Merriam couldn't have had a more disappointing child fall from her if she'd tried. Raven. Even her name sounded like something that a commoner would call their child.

Roger had been lavish with his gifts to her, however. He'd not only given Merriam a tennis bracelet with a dozen diamonds on it, but also dozens of roses, as well as a whole year at her favorite spa. She'd loved it, and had even considered having a second child for him.

Since there was a nanny to take care of the brat, Merriam went about her life without much change. Then, when she felt like she looked like she had before Raven had messed up her body, she went to the club, planning to show off not just the spa card she'd gotten, but also the bracelet.

"Oh, you know why he got you that spa membership, don't you?" She told Meggie, one of the women she used to hang out with, that it had been a gift for having a child. "No. It's to get you into shape again. My husband actually told me that there is this group of golfers that he hangs out with that talks about that sort of thing. What to give a wife when she has a child. What to give a mistress when you're breaking it off with her. Things like that. A spa gift is right up there on the top of the list for all kinds of things. He just wants you to be in shape so that you're ready for the next kid to pop out for him."

"That's ridiculous. I'm in the best shape of my life." She wasn't, however. The girdle that she had on was pinching her in a way that she wasn't sure she could even eat. "He'd better not be doing that to me. I swear to you if he is…. Well, you might not see him around for a while."

After lunch, not only did she confront Roger, who, of course, denied it, but she also threw a great many of his treasures at him. Damn the man, making her look like a fool. Well, he'd never done that again, and she made sure that every time she was late or suspected that she might be pregnant, she took care of it immediately. There was no way she was going to be the talk of the club again. She was an Addington, for Christ's sake.

Sitting in her cell, she picked up her blanket. There was no point in asking for a fresh one. They'd just toss it at her in the cell she was confined to and tell her that she wasn't getting another one for a week. At home, she had demanded clean sheets daily, as all Addingtons should.

Merriam was lonely. Of course, she'd never admit that to anyone but herself. She was used to being the center of attention everywhere she went. It made her feel better than others when she was able to pick up the tab for lunch or dinner when out and never look at the amount. She didn't leave tips for people who had the privilege of waiting on her. That made her feel superior to everyone that she was with. If the staff wanted extra money, then find a job that paid better. It wasn't her responsibility to pay people for a job they chose over a real one.

Her house had been her pride and joy. Having people over so that they could look at the things that had been collected by past generations of Addingtons gave her a sense of pride that she couldn't explain. She supposed that it had something to do with the fact that they were wealthy enough not to have to sell off heirlooms when they were broke. There was an endless supply of money, and she used it to her advantage over others as often as she could.

Looking around the cell, she was depressed to see that nothing had been done to it while she'd been gone. Once a week—only once a week—they came in and tidied up. That only meant that they emptied her trash can and ran a quick mop over the concrete floor. The toilet that hung from the wall was her responsibility. Merriam had no more idea how to clean a commode than she did how to make a bed. Those things were done for her because of who she was.

Wondering what she was going to do now, Merriam decided that she was going to continue with her list of demands from Roger. First and foremost, he was going to go back to the way things were when she was in charge. He had no doubt tasted a little freedom with her gone, but she'd be nipping that in the bud as soon as she could. There would also be no more time spent with that bastard child of Raven's. He obviously thought that playing in the dirt was going to be all right with her.

"Think again." Picking up her pencil and paper, she began writing things down that she needed. Better treatment, while she was stuck here, was at the top. Also, he was going to visit her regularly. What would people think if he were to just abandon her like he seemed to think that he could? "Again, Roger, think again. I won't allow that."

When lunch was brought to her, Merriam told them, for the millionth time, that she wanted a nice garden-fresh salad with the dressing on the side, a glass of wine, as well as some fresh, not frozen, fruit. Like always, they simply walked away, leaving her a sandwich again, along with the ever present bag of chips and two bottles of water. This shit was getting old.

~*~

Chandler wanted to tell Molly that he was going to find them a house on his own, but almost as soon as they pulled up in front of the mansion, no other word for it, he could see that Sasha loved it. He did too, but it was nothing that he could afford right now. If ever.

"Mom bought all of my uncles homes." Chandler asked Molly when she'd done that. "I don't know when, but I know that you get to pick the one that you want first. She said that she got this amazing deal and that you and Sasha would be happy being close to everyone. I like it too. I can't wait until I can watch Pip for you."

"We're going to go see her after this. I guess she's a tiny little thing." Molly and Sasha wandered ahead of them as Molly told Sasha about Pip. About how much she liked practicing with her because she was going to be a big sister soon. Chandler took the closed door to the right of where they'd gone and stood there staring at the room.

It was an office made for a man who liked to read. There were windows all around the room, and floor to ceiling shelves. A ladder on each side of the room slid along the top so that he could even get books from the very top of the shelf should he need too. The desk that was there was huge too. Something that a person could have sex on should they want.

Shaking that thought out of his head for the moment, Chandler walked further into the room. There was an envelope on the desk with his name on it, and he picked it up, recognizing the handwriting as his brother's. Opening it, several keys fell out, and he bent to pick them up as he read the note.

"Chandler, I love this house for you. Several reasons come to mind. In the back of the property, there is a secondary entrance and a really nice building that you can use as your office for your practice. You'll have to take a run out there and see what I mean about how it's perfect. Also, you're within walking distance from not just our home, but Mom and Dad's too. Molly is most excited about that part. She's head over heels in love with little Pip." He wondered again what they'd name the child when they took her in but continued reading instead. "Raven had Molly take you to the house because she figured that you'd not be upset with her. I want you to know how happy I am that we can do this for you and the others. As soon as we can convince them, we're going to see about getting Mom and Dad a better home as well. The house we grew up in is falling apart around their ears. Did you notice that Mom puts out pans to catch the leaks when it rains still? Not good."

He had noticed that, and had thought the same thing—that they needed something not just smaller, but also newer. Mom was still cooking on a stove that only had one burner, and it was difficult for her to make a meal now with all of them there. Chandler sat down at the desk and read the rest of the note.

"I want you to know something that I hope you already know. That I love you. I don't think we say that to each other enough. But buying these houses for you and the others, we're not doing it so that you can feel as if we're ashamed of you, or that we're trying to make you take something that would make you feel as if you owe us anything. We're doing this because we want you safe, happy, and not in debt for the rest of your life.

"Go to college, Chandler. Fulfill your dream of being a veterinarian. The house is yours whether you go to college or not, but you don't have to worry about money or anything else so long as we have it. Not for any other reason than we love you all."

He was still sitting there, thinking about what Sawyer had said when Molly and Sasha joined him. Handing her the letter from his brother, he asked Molly to show him the bedrooms. They were on the second floor, and she told him that she'd already picked out the one that he should keep for her when she came to visit him. Chandler loved this kid.

When Sasha joined them, he could tell that she'd been crying. When she laid her head on his chest when she came to him, Chandler told her that he loved her. Pulling away from him when Molly tugged on her, they entered what he could only assume was the master bedroom.

"Holy fuck." He felt his face heat up when Molly scolded him. "Look at this place. I mean, seriously, we could live in here and never have to see the rest of the house, I think."

"That would be a total waste of space, don't you think, Uncle Chandler?" She went to the closet, then came out. "Okay, I've changed my mind. Look at these closets. There is one for each of you. And I could move in here, and you'd never know it. I love this house."

"I do too." Chandler looked at Sasha when she spoke. "This is a house that every person in the world dreams of having, yet never gets. A house that would be something that we can use for the rest of our lives. Bringing families here. Our family. Raising not just Pip but other children as well. I would, if you don't mind, love to live in this house and grow old with you, Chandler Bishop."

"I would like nothing better than to give you this house from my family as a place that we can live in." She laughed with him. "While we're on the subject of making sure that we have a roof over our heads, will you marry me, Sasha Harvard? Be the wife that I've always thought that I'd love and cherish?"

"I will." Molly began shouting and whooping it up when she heard Sasha's answer. Laughing at the antics that only a kid could do, Sasha turned to the little girl and spoke to her. "You must be my bridesmaid, Molly. I'd have it no other way than to have you standing up there with the rest of my new family."

"It's a deal." She was still shouting about how cool it was that Sasha was going to be her aunt. Then when she stopped long enough to speak again, it made her more excited. "That means that Pip will be my cousin, doesn't it?"

"It does."

Molly took off for parts unknown in the house as Chandler was led from room to room with Sasha. Once in a while, Molly would come back to say something, but all in all, they were alone to make decisions. Chandler was just nervous about how they were going to fill out the house, much less where to put the beds they didn't have in it.

Before they finished up on the third floor of the big house, his family came by. Once, when they'd been looking at the way the closets all seemed to have been put in recently, Sawyer asked him what they had decided. He then realized that though they weren't blood related, his brother and Molly had the same enthusiastic *whooping*. Chandler was happy that he'd been able to make their day. His whole life was happy now.

They came bearing gifts, his family did. Not only did they have a new bedroom set, but there was a mattress for the new baby bed for Pip. Holding the little girl made him feel good, so when Sasha looked at her in his arms, he handed her to her new momma so that she could feel just as good.

"She's so tiny, isn't she?" Sasha sat down in the only piece of furniture in the living room. The beautiful rocking chair had been a gift from his parents. "She's beautiful, don't you think, Chandler?"

"Yes. And when she's awake, she looks right at you as if she knows just who you are and what you're thinking." Sasha nodded. "Are we going to name her Pip? Or can you think of another name and we can just call her that? I'm partial to calling her Pip. It suits her for some reason."

"I think it does as well. But I'll have to think on that a little bit. What's your mom's name?" He told her that it was Serendipity, but she was called Sippy. "That will make a good middle name for her. I don't want to name her for my mother. She's not the type of person that would be happy having anything or anyone named for her. How about Emmaline? That's a good strong name, don't you think? Emmaline Serendipity Bishop. Yes, I love that. How about you?"

"I love it too. She'll be able to go by anything she wants when she gets old enough to pick if Pip isn't anything that she likes." Sasha told him that he thought with everyone calling her Pip, she'd keep it. "I hope so. It's a good name for someone that has started out life just this side of bad things going down."

He didn't want to say death, but it was there on

his mind. If he had been only a few minutes more or hadn't gone running with his brother, she would have died. Shaking his head, he didn't want to think about all the things that might have happened to her had he not found her. Chandler knew that it was fate. Just as it was fate that he fall in love with Sasha. Not only was he a husband to be, but a father too. Dad. Chandler was a dad now.

"I have some things that I'd like to give you and the other boys." Chandler told Holly that she didn't have to give them anything. That they were just happy that she hung out with them. "I sort of knew you were going to say something like that. So I had it all packed up and brought over anyway. You each get a nice truckload of furniture that was in my house."

"You've sold your house?" She grinned at him, and he looked around. "This was your house, wasn't it? Why, you sly woman, you. Why would you do that? I'm sure that there are other houses, much smaller ones that Sasha and I could have moved into."

"I'm sure there are. But you're the only one with a baby that didn't have a home. Sawyer has their home, and I want you to have this one." About the time he was hugging her, the semi, not just a truck, pulled up in front of the house. He asked her about it. "You're the one that assumed it was a pick-up truck. I only said it was a truck. Come on, let's get that sucker unloaded, and see what you have."

Every time he pulled something off the truck, it seemed like there was twice that many more pieces to remove. Not only did they have a really beautiful dining room set, but also living room furniture as well as things for them to use in the kitchen. When a woman by the name of Trudy said she'd set up the kitchen, Chandler had an idea that they had a cook too.

Sasha was directing his brothers around so that the furniture was in the correct rooms. She kept telling them that they could move it later. Laughing every time Sawyer went by him with another load, grumbling about moving shit, he thought of all the fun he was going to have in their new home. This might be one of the best days of his life, Chandler thought. A home, a wife, and family right here helping out.

At nearly seven o'clock, they were called to dinner. He didn't have any idea what might be served to them, as he'd not seen a single one of them rush off to the grocery store. But when they sat down at the table that had only just gotten chairs around it, they were given not just baked potatoes, green beans, and rolls, but thick steaks as they came off the grill right outside of the dining room. Chandler thought that he could certainly get used to this.

Sasha leaned over to him while he was eating and told him that she needed to talk to him about her family.

Asking her if it was bad, she only had to nod. He didn't expect anything less than that. Having a terrible family seemed to be the norm when it came to wives for them. Telling her that they'd take care of them, he also told her that she needed to tell them all about it.

"I will. Tomorrow. Not today. This is for family, and I want to have more fun with moving into this place with them all helping." He did too and told her that. "You know, it's really nice having family around, isn't it?"

Roger, who had come to help too, said that he agreed with her on that. He didn't know how badly he'd had it until now. "These Bishops, they know just how to treat someone and give them a boost up. I've certainly been enjoying living with them all. And I have good friends now in Saul and Sippy. Something that I don't think I've ever had before."

As they finished up their meal with the promise of dessert when the truck was emptied, they all worked harder for the chance to sit down and have some pie. Sasha said she was going to gain a ton if this kept up, the way they ate. He'd have to talk to her soon about changing her. Then she and Pip would be safer if he wasn't here. Not to mention, she'd never have to worry about gaining weight again.

Chapter 5

Pulling her cell phone out of her pocket, Sasha put it away. There wasn't any way that she was going to answer a call from her mother right now. There was just too much going on. Not to mention, she didn't want to speak to her.

The bedroom that they were going to share was coming along nicely. Holly helped her with putting the things like she wanted them in the room. The bed with the back to the large window did seem to make the room look larger. The curtains that were there when they looked around the house earlier were, of course, a perfect match to the blanket and other items that went with the room. Too bad they didn't have a mattress just yet.

"I had this linen set made for me when I was first widowed. I thought that the colors would calm me enough that I'd sleep better. I never did sleep in this room after my husband passed on. It was just too much for me." Sasha told her that she was sorry. "I'm not. I get to know now that I picked out a perfect set for my two favorite people. That's one of the reasons that I wanted to unpack the things I've had in storage for so long. To see them used by young couples starting out. The others are getting the same kind of furniture. But this set, it was mine and my husband's, and I simply love it. As I do you."

"I love you too, Holly. I can see why Raven has nothing but wonderful things to say about you. You don't hold back unless you have to. Even then, you're a straight shooter. I love that about you."

"Thank you, my dear. I'm noticing that you're just like myself and Raven. Tell me about your mother. I'm sure that it's more than what I've read from the report I had about you." She asked her if she'd had her investigated. "Yes. And I'm not the least bit sorry for it either. You are going to be a part of the family that my granddaughter and great-granddaughter are a part of. I won't have them hurt when the shit hits the fan. Not that I would have kept you from being a part of this wonderful loud group, but I would have kept a closer eye on you. You know about my daughter-in-law, Merriam."

"I do. Raven told me some of it. Molly did as well.

And I kind of know Merriam. She's in jail right now, awaiting trial." Holly told her that it couldn't come soon enough for her. "No, I don't think that I would want it dragged out either. Roger is your son."

"Yes. I'm not usually one to say I-told-you-so, but I did try to warn him about her. She was just too slick for me. And the fact that everything she does hinges on the fact that as an Addington, that's the way it should be done used to drive me bonkers." They both laughed. "Your mother, she's not hurt, is she?"

"No. I don't know that she ever was, to be honest. When she fell that time, in a department store, I could never figure out why she'd been there in the first place, unless she was looking for a job. Still, I don't think that they'd hire her. But she was there, shopping, she told us. No way could she have afforded anything there." Holly asked again what had happened. "She was found lying on the floor in the bathroom. The floor was wet, but that looked to me like she'd poured water there. According to her, she'd fallen on the floor and hurt her back. They told us, my brother, sister, and me, that Mother's injuries were consistent with a slip and a fall. But that they didn't know how she'd hurt her back."

"She's been in a wheelchair since then, I read." Sasha told her that she'd been faking it in a wheelchair since then. "You have any proof?"

"No. How I wish I did. She has these doctors that

agree with the fact that her injury could be something that her mind is making up for her. I believe that my mother is well aware of what she's doing. Not only is she getting a monthly check to cover her being hurt, but they also make sure that she has help to exercise her legs, in the event that she ever decides to get up moving again. She also has the latest wheelchair, a car that can carry her lazy ass around, as well as all the drugs she needs."

"You don't think she needs any of that." Sasha told her that she didn't think her mother needed the drugs for sure. "Why get them then? Who's footing the bill for that?"

"Again, I have no proof, but I do think she's making a killing off the market for them." Holly whistled. "I know. It's a horrible thing to think about your own mother, but damn it, she's hurting the company that has to foot the bill for her scam. This isn't the first time she's done something like this either. I believe that is why my dad left her. She was trying to drag him into things that he didn't want to have any part of."

"Your mother, did she ever try to sell off your abilities?" Sasha nodded. "I thought as much. There was an article in one of the papers that I was given that said how you could find lost souls and money. I never understood why anyone would advertise something like that. You must have had every person in the world coming for you."

"I did. And not just the living either. The dead thought that since it was out there, then I would have no problem finding their money and giving it to their families. It didn't work that way for me. I would only be able to tell the police where their bodies were, and then they'd disappear." Holly asked her what was different now. "I forgot to mention it. I've been promoted, they told me. Not only can I tell the police where they've been buried or whatever, but I can also find things that they might have taken from someone, like robbing a bank so that the money can be returned to whomever."

Glancing over Holly's shoulder, she saw the nice looking older man. She didn't want to tell Holly that she thought her husband was there, but it seemed so cruel not to tell her. Holly asked her who she was seeing when she caught her looking.

"I don't know. But I do think that your husband is here." Holly shook her head. "You don't have to speak to him, Holly. He doesn't look as if he's going to cause you any harm. I think he just wants to see you."

Holly turned slowly and asked where he was. Reaching for her hand when she put hers toward her, Sasha was startled when the man became solid enough for both of them to see him. He smiled at them, and Sasha was happy to see that he'd been made over somewhat. That, however he died, he didn't look like he was dead right now.

"Roger?" He nodded and put out his hand. They, of course, couldn't touch, but it was so lovely to see them pretending to hold each other's hands. "I've missed you so much. I wish every day that you were here."

"I'm all right where I am, love. Besides, had I still been there with you, how on earth would you have had as many adventures as you've had? I've seen you on your trips. I'm so happy that you enjoy them with our great-granddaughter."

"Molly would have loved you so much, Roger. You know that, don't you?" He said that he already loved her. "You've missed so much, my love. We're going to be great-grandparents again."

"You've kept me up to date, Holly. Every time you come out to the gravesite where I am, you tell me everything. I'm the envy of every person on this side because you bring pictures with you for me to see. I see them." She laughed and cried at the same time. "Raven hasn't been out to see me as much, but I understand why. That mother of hers should be shot, I think. And that Molly? I just can't stand that I can't touch her or talk to her once in a while. But she shares with me. Her secrets and her laughter. It's about all a man in my position could ask for when he's moved on."

Sasha stayed with them. Honestly, she thought that she was getting to see what long term true love was like. Also, she was afraid that if she let go of Holly's hand, she'd not be able to see her husband. That more than anything was the reason that she held so tightly to the elderly woman's hand.

"I must go, my love. It's draining to stay like this to speak to you. I should like, if the lady Sasha doesn't mind, to do this again sometime. I so love talking to you." Holly looked at her, and Sasha nodded. "Good. That's just wonderful. The next time you come to see me, my heart, don't forget those pictures. And a blanket. I don't wish you to be joining me none too soon when there are babies coming."

"I won't forget, Roger. I love you and miss you so very much." He told her that he loved her, too, as he faded away. Holly turned to her when he was gone, tears still fresh in her eyes. "What you did for me and Roger just now, it makes my heart just a little fuller. So what I'm going to do is take care of your mother for you. I won't go to the extremes as Raven would, but we'll get her taken care of. You just wait and see."

"You don't have to do that." Holly told her that she did, and not just for the time she'd spent with Roger. "She'll get her just desserts, I know it. It might take time, but I'm sure she'll get it."

"She will. Now, I have to make a couple of phone calls. I need to get my attorney on this. Brooks will think that he's a special agent when I talk to him. Oh, he'll love this as much as I'm going to."

When she left her there, sitting on the half folded linens that were for their bed when it arrived, Sasha laughed. It was going to be fun to see her mother get her comeuppance. Her brother and sister as well. They weren't terrible, not like their mother was, but they needed to see the error of their ways as well.

Pearl's way of getting things on sale was to steal them. She got away with it because she was so overweight. Her sister had told her once that no one would accuse her of doing it because she'd say that they were biased because of her being slightly overweight. She was more than slightly, but Sasha didn't say anything to her about it. Basically, Pearl was right. No one would want to get into a lawsuit over a few articles of clothing that would cost them a great deal less than a lawsuit would.

Zack. Zack was into everything illegal. The only thing that Sasha thought he didn't do was dealing drugs. Why would he want to take away from Mom's business? She thought. They were all three doing things rather than working a good job.

Pearl did work, but it was in customer service online. No way would anyone trust her to be out front with people. Pearl could be nice when it suited her, which wasn't often. Around Mom, Sasha had noticed she was as good and kind as she could be. Sasha never understood why she was, but that was her.

Zack was a prick—a jackass as well. As the old saying would go, he'd take the pennies off a dead man's eyes if he found them. His job consisted of trying to be one step ahead of the cops, something that he failed at more often than not. He'd only moved back in with Mom because her house was better than the streets or jail, and she had food around all the time. Both of them needed a reality check, and she wanted them to have it. In the worst sort of way.

Finishing up the towels that had arrived, Sasha looked at the baby bed that had come too. It was so sweet and pink. Not over the top pink, but enough to know that a little girl was sleeping there. She and Chandler both had decided that she'd sleep in their room for a while, just until they got used to having an infant around. Neither of them had all that much experience with a baby, so she was glad that they were doing this together.

When she made her way downstairs a few minutes later, she found that most of the house was finished up and that they were all enjoying the television that hadn't been there earlier. Sasha wondered if any of them cared who won the preseason football game they were watching.

"We're Ohio, all the way."

She asked him why he'd be rooting for the Browns.

That got a lot of groans from them all, but Quincey was impressed that she knew who they were. "I watch the game. I love football."

"You just love all the testosterone that is floating around when a game is on, that's all." They were nudging each other about the joke that Quincey had made. "Will you make tailgate food for us, Sasha?"

"Okay, dick weed. From nineteen forty-six to sixty-two, they had Paul Brown. He's the man that they named not only the team after, but the stadium that they had as well. Which was torn down in November of sixty-six. From sixty-three to seventy, they had Blanton Collier. Nick Skorich from seventy-one until seventy-four. Forrest Gregg was from seventy-five to seventy-seven. Since nineteen-ninety, they've had fourteen more coaches, all of them lasting just long enough to be traded for someone else. Do you want me to name those for you as well?" No one said a word. "There are other stats I can give you too. How about the Bengals or Ohio State? I know a great deal about them, too, including how many times they've gone to and won what used to be called the Rose Bowl."

"Damn, girl." Dwayne grinned at Quincey. "I think she's a true fan, buddy. When the game comes on next week, you're making the food so that she can be in here with us when the game is on. Hot damn that was epic."

They all got a kick out of her knowledge of the

teams. She loved football and was glad that she could be one of them when they watched the games. Sasha would make some food for them when they came over. She thought that she'd very much like having them all over for game day, as much as she loved the games.

Bonding with his brothers. It was something that she'd never thought that she'd be able to do with any man. But having them in her corner, she thought, was what was going to be best for her. Picking up Pip and holding her, Sasha thought that she could be a momma and a fan of sports too. *Just wait until baseball season starts,* she thought. Sasha knew much more about the Reds than any of them, she'd bet.

"Momma is going to make them sit up and take notice, you watch and see." Pip looked at her, and Sasha thought that she smiled at her. "That's my girl. You and I, we have a great deal to learn about each other. Also, I need to tell your grandma Holly about Melinda. Perhaps we can clear up that too. Wouldn't you like to know about the man that killed her? I would."

The rest of the game was a great deal of shouting and yelling. She realized about halftime that they didn't care for either team all that much, but just wanted to watch a game. She'd have to remember that when they came back to watch games with them. They were all diehard Browns fans, as well as the Indians baseball team from Cleveland. Sasha was going to have fun with them all.

~*~

Katie hated this. The doctors were to show up in forty minutes, and she didn't want to blow this. Zack had left her, too, saying that he didn't want to be caught on camera. She knew why. Her son was in trouble again. Her precious baby boy was a trouble maker from way back.

Pearl was in her room, sobbing. The wedding hadn't gone as well as she'd hoped. The dress, of course, didn't fit, and when she'd had to show up in something less fitting, they'd had a good time at her expense, telling her that the skirt she had on wasn't anything new and that they didn't see any change in her weight. Katie had tried to tell her, but who listened to their mom nowadays? No one, it seemed.

She wished that she had more of an idea about what they were going to be asking her. Basically, she wanted to make sure that she could answer the questions and not get pissy with them. That would blow up in her face if she did that.

Calm, she told herself. She needed to not just be calm but pitiful as well. She'd done this so much in the past in front of her kids that she thought that she could do it in her sleep. That, she knew, would trip her up too. Being much too confident in her ability to pull the wool over their eyes.

When the knock at the door made her jump, Katie scolded herself while going to the door. People who couldn't use their legs didn't jump up from their chairs. Moving toward the door, she gave herself a much needed pep talk. Katie wanted to slam it back in its place when she opened it and saw Sasha there.

"I don't have time for you today. You come back tomorrow." There was an elderly woman with her whom she didn't want there either. "Sasha, I've been trying to call you for days now. Showing up unannounced is not what I wanted. We'll talk later. Go away, and I'll call you."

"Mrs. Addington is part of the panel that is talking to you today. I'm her driver and friend. If you toss us out, Mother dear, then you will forfeit everything." Katie wasn't just rolled back out of the way by her daughter but shoved back hard enough to knock things around on the table behind her. "Where are the other two? Speaking of the other two, I wanted you to know that I met my sister Melinda."

Katie felt the world spin out of control for several seconds. When things settled, she had her head down and between her knees with someone holding her there. Not ready yet to face her daughter, she told her that she had no idea what she was talking about.

"I only have the two daughters, Sasha. One of them is heartbroken right now, the other has broken my heart." She was released and saw that Mrs. Addington had been the one holding her down. "Thank you. I'm sure that Sasha wouldn't have helped her poor, disabled mother out."

"I'm sure if she had one, Sasha would have been right there." It took her a moment to figure out that the elderly lady was telling her that she didn't believe her story about being crippled up. "Melinda said that you were her mother. Also, that you put her last name as Harvard before you got around to putting her up for adoption. Now that I see you, I can see that you figured you had a good reason for doing something so heinous. Why would you do that to your own child, I wonder?"

"I still have no idea what you're talking about." Katie desperately wanted to change the subject. Looking at her daughter as she sat on the couch and ate a bag of her chips, Katie wanted to snatch them away from her. "Don't you have your own place that you could make yourself at home in? I'd very much like it if you were to stop snooping around my home."

"My home." She asked her what she was talking about. "I purchased this rental this morning. It was a good buy. I will be raising your rent here too. So when you start making out the monthly check for your rent, you'll want to make sure you get my name right. I'm Sasha Bishop now."

"You changed your name? What was wrong with Harvard? Nothing. You always were too uppity to have been around us much." Sasha told her that she'd gotten married. "Married? You? Does he have any idea what you say you can do? Does he know that you claim you can see ghosts?"

"He can as well."

When the door was knocked on again, Katie just barely caught herself from getting up and answering it. Looking at Mrs. Addington when she laughed, Katie had an idea that she knew everything that was going on.

Sasha opened the door to the other panel members that were supposed to be there. Katie wanted to ask for them to come another day. She was so upset right now that she was sure to make a mistake. All her mind could center on was the fact that Sasha was married, knew about Melinda, and she owned her house. How was any of that possible?

"She's dead then." Everyone turned to look at Katie when something occurred to her, and she blurted it out. "You said that you met this Melinda person. And that she told you that I was her mother. First of all, what proof do you have that she's telling the truth? Not to mention, you're taking the word of a ghost over your own mother."

"Excuse me?" She might have been introduced to

the man, but she couldn't for the life of her remember his name. "What do you mean, she's dead? Who's dead, and why is that relevant to this case?"

"It's not. I mean, I was having a conversation with my daughter here, and she brought something up that's not true." Her face flushed hotly. "She's forever telling lies, this one. She even went for a long time telling people that she could see ghosts. I think you can understand why I'd not like her here when this is going on. She'll try to make me look bad in front of you."

"Mrs. Bishop is a friend of Mrs. Addington. And as such, she's a friend of this board. If you have an issue with her being here, then I would like to point out that if we don't do this today, we no longer have to give you a date and time to show up. Which is it going to be, Ms. Harvard?" Katie told them that today was fine. "Good. I'm glad to hear that. As for her seeing ghosts? Well, the only thing I have to say about that is, Mrs. Bishop and her husband have been extremely helpful of late to not just the local police department, but also the FBI. In the last several days, both departments have been able to close several cases thanks to them."

"Yes, of course. But I don't believe that she's married to anyone either." The man huffed at her and asked her if *that* was relevant to the case. "No. I'm just flustered, and she's making me that way. I don't want to mess up in answering your questions because she is here, making me upset."

"If you're telling the truth, there should be no reason whatsoever that you would mess up. You are telling the truth, aren't you?" Katie looked at the man. There was something about him that made her want to tell him that she was lying. Tell him that it had all been a scam. There wasn't a thing wrong with her. "Ms. Harvard, your nose is bleeding. You shouldn't fight so hard."

She knew then that he was trying his best to make her say things. Katie didn't know what it was called, this thing he was doing to her, but she did know that she had beat him once at his game, and she'd do so again. Biting her lower lip, she concentrated on what was going on around her. Making her lip sore was going to be a small price to pay for getting out of this unscathed.

"Now, Ms. Harvard, are you ready to begin?" Nodding at him, she waited for him to start. "I'm sorry, Ms. Harvard. Since this is being recorded, both vocally and on video, you will need to answer each question as it is asked of you. Let's begin again. Are you ready to begin?"

"Yes. I'm ready. Does Sasha have to be here? I'm only asking because she'll try very hard to trip me up." The man told her again if she was telling the truth, there shouldn't be anything for her to worry about. "All right. Let's get this over with so that I can get you people out of my house."

"My house." Growling at Sasha, she wanted to slap the piss out of her. "Mother, can you tell me if you can walk? Get up out of your chair?"

Katie looked at the man. When he nodded, she looked at her daughter again. "No. I cannot. And you would know that if you came around more often. When was the last time you were here, Sasha? Since you came to check on your own mother?"

"Months. Perhaps years. I don't know. Don't care either." Sasha had always been so cold to her. "When you said that you couldn't walk, does that mean that you have no feeling in your legs? Or back? Tell us what it is that keeps you from getting up and say...checking on the mail?"

"I fell. I was in the bathroom at one of the department stores, and there was water on the floor that I didn't see until I was falling. I think perhaps I hit my head, but when I woke up, there were people all around me." Mrs. Addington asked her why she was in that particular store. "I was buying a gift for my son. It was close to his birthday."

"Zack's birthday was six weeks after you fell. Why don't you try that one again?" Sasha was going to fuck her over if she didn't shut the fuck up. "And what on earth do you suppose Zack would have wanted from that store? I mean, it's a women's clothing and accessories store, correct? I don't think my brother wears makeup. I looked, and that is by far the cheapest thing in the place."

"They were having a sale." Were they? Katie had no idea. So turning in her chair, she looked at the two other people that had come in with the man. "Do you have anything to ask of me, gentlemen? It seems my daughter is taking up most of your time here."

"She said that she'd help us, and I think she's doing a bang up job." The man smiled at her, and that was when she saw his fangs. "You'll answer her truthfully, won't you, Sally Harvard?"

It was there again. Whatever he was doing to her, she couldn't lie to anyone. So instead of trying to get out of saying the wrong thing, she told them that she wanted them to go. The vampire just laughed. Then he told Sasha to proceed.

"Why did you give up Melinda?" She didn't, she told her. "Then why was she not living with us after she was born? What did you do to her?"

"I didn't want another mouth to feed. Damn it, do you have any idea how much it cost me just to feed you three? A lot, let me tell you." Sasha asked her again why Melinda had not lived with them. "I sold her off to the highest bidder. I made a great deal of money off that too."

Slapping her hand over her mouth, she looked at the men and Sasha. That right there, admitting that she'd sold off one of her kids, was enough to get her in deep shit. Katie wanted them gone. All of them.

"I have had enough of this. I want you all to get out of here right now." No one moved as she made her way to the door. "Did you hear me? I said I want you to leave this house right now."

"Too bad. So you sold off Melinda to someone that gave you a great deal of money. How much?" She had to tell her the amount and the date when it had happened. "She was only a baby when you sold her. Do you know who the person was you sold her to? Have you any idea what was done to her when she was murdered? She was, by the way. Murdered so that her baby would die as well. I have her, Mother. Pip is what we call her. She'll never meet you, I'm so happy to say, but she'll be raised as my daughter. Also, she'll be able to see ghosts. Can you walk?"

"Yes."

The room seemed to explode with movement around her. Dizzy, she put her head down again and sat there as feet, many of them, were moving within her sight. Not lifting her head, even when she'd been told to do so, seemed like a brilliant idea.

"Mother, look at me."

Lifting her head up finally, she looked at her daughter. There was something about her that made Katie cringe away from her when she reached for her. Sasha just smiled when she spoke to her. Her voice did not reflect the smile that was on her voice.

"You'll be going to jail in about ten minutes. As well as Pearl and Zack. There are enough drugs and merchandise in this place to open not just a pharmacy, but a boutique as well. I suppose you have a reason for that as well." Nodding, she watched as Sasha sat down on the couch that was now empty of the other people. "Well? Do you have anything to say to me?"

"I loathe you, Sasha. Hate you with every fiber of my being. Why did it matter to you that we were getting a little extra on the side? Tell me. Does it make you feel like you won something? To take everything away that we've worked so hard to get?" She asked her what she'd actually done to work for it. "You sit there all high and mighty, telling me not only that you're married, but that you have enough money to buy broken down houses so that your mother will have to live on the streets. Your brother and sister are—"

"You won't be living on the streets, Mother. You'll be going to jail. For a very long time. You know, I had only planned on having you arrested for insurance fraud. But when you told me how you were so callus in the way you rid yourself of Melinda, I decided that you didn't deserve anything at all from me. Especially after I spoke to Melinda about how she was sold off and to whom."

"Am I supposed to be sorry for it? I'm not. I'm sorry that I didn't sell you off as well. You're nothing to me. Don't come around me again." Sasha was still laughing as she left the house. "I hate you. I hate you to the very core of my being."

The police came into the room as Sasha was leaving. When Katie was pulled from the chair that she'd been in for years, she stood there while her rights were read to her. Katie watched as they dragged Pearl out of her room. Her face was a mess from the tears that she'd shed. That, too, Katie wanted to think was Sasha's fault. The fucking bitch had turned her back on her own family, and Katie hoped she regretted it for the rest of her life.

Chapter 6

"I found something that might help you guys." Gunner came into the room where he'd been working like he'd been there for a while. "Are you all right?"

Chandler nodded and said that he'd forgotten the time. "I was looking over the classes that I can take, and also making a list of ones that I think I can test out of. Doc Joe told me that there is at least a year or two worth of them that I can skip. What did you find?"

"There is this guy that is making a lot of noise about how he's innocent. He's a mobster from way back, and he's strongly suggesting to all the agencies that they're not to step on his land with any kind of equipment." Chandler asked him if he thought he might murder a mother and child. "Oh yeah. He'd not have a moment's hesitation in doing something like that. If even half of what I've found from missing persons is true, I'd say that he has a very good reason not to allow anyone even within a mile of his place. But I have my ways."

"What did you do?" Instead of answering him, he handed him several pictures. It took him a moment to figure out what they were, but when he did, Chandler looked at him. "Are these aerial shots of his land? Is this even legal?"

"No. But then I don't usually play by the rules when I want something. The blank spots that you can see in the lower half of the pictures are what I *was* assuming are bodies. The second set of pictures are x-ray pictures of the same plots. Once I was able to show some people what I had found, they used their infrared cameras and did a little more detail. As you can see, there are bones in those blank spots now." Not just a couple of them either, Chandler noticed, but at least a dozen. "They only need to have reasonable cause to just say fuck it and go in. This is going to give them that right."

"But you're not sure that this is him? I mean, this is amazing. I'm sure that it will close a great many cases. You did a great thing here." Gunner said that the people he was helping, they wanted to use Sasha to sort them out. "You mean find out who they might be. You'd have to ask her that, Gunner. I mean, I'd do it, no problem. But I'm still having a little trouble with focusing the people into telling me what I need to know from them."

"Sasha needs to be asked about what?"

She came into the room and handed him Pip. Chandler thought that she got bigger every day. When Gunner took her from him, he tried to console himself with the fact that she was his daughter, and Gunner didn't see her as often as he did. Gunner explained to Sasha what he needed.

"I would love to help you out with that. In fact, I was just coming to talk to Chandler about a man that is in our kitchen. He said that he knows you, Gunner."

"Do you know his name?" She told him what she knew. "I don't know anyone by that name. Is he dressed as a real person, or is he dressed like I am?"

"Real person? I guess I can see where you'd think that you're not real in those fatigues. But you're a real person to me. He's dressed in a pair of men's pajamas that are much too large for him. One slipper, and he looks like he has had his throat slit." Gunner stood up and asked her what his name was again. "Holloway. That's all he gave me."

"Can you send him away? He's one of my targets, someone that was selling our shit to another country." Sasha nodded, then left them. Gunner looked at him. "Do you think this is going to happen often? Where someone from my checkered past is going to come here for some reason?"

"I don't know, to be honest with you. I just found

out that when a person, the dead, is really pissed off and has a lot of built up anger, they can harm humans. Like the guy that went after Sasha. He was able to use a bat on her when she found his wife at the bottom of a lake." Gunner said that he was glad for the information. "Yeah, me too. I thought that it was a vampire or something, but it turns out, he was one fucking pissed off dead man."

Sasha rejoined them. "He's gone. No biggie there. I can send them away so that they don't seek revenge. That was what he was here for, by the way." She smiled at Gunner. "If you could give me a list of things that I need to look for on the dead that come around for you, I can narrow down whether or not you need to come around or not. I'm thinking that if they come in fatigues, they might have died next to you, correct?"

"No." When she nodded and didn't say anymore, he thought that Gunner looked relieved. "They want to know if you can be ready as soon as the team is ready to go in a couple of days. That would be great. I'll take you out tomorrow so you can have a look around the area. It'll be from a distance, but you'll have a better idea of what we're looking at area-wise. They want to get a start on the land as soon as possible. However, it'll be before the sun comes up. Mr. Gauthier will still be in bed at that time. They have to serve him about what they're doing, but we're not allowed to make him aware of it before we begin."

"You work for these people." This time Gunner did nothing more than stare at Sasha. Chandler felt a cold chill run over his skin at the blank look on his brother's face. "I need something, Gunner. Even if it's only to tell me that you will be my direct contact on this. I don't want to be left holding the bag when it turns out there are not only no bodies out there, but that I'll the one they think started this thing as a sort of revenge."

"You will report to me, and me only, unless I tell you otherwise. I would like for you to wear dark clothing so that you won't stand out from the others there. There will be a camera crew there, but they know to blur out your face." She thanked him for that. "I know that you have a carry permit. I would like it if you were armed, as well as wearing a vest under your shirt."

"I don't have a weapon. I left it at my other place." He said that he'd get it for her. "Thanks. Gunner, are you expecting trouble from me being there?"

"Not from you being there, no. But I always expect the worst when it comes to dealing with pieces of shit like Gauthier." Gunner stood up. "I'll be here at four in the morning. If you could be ready, I'll make sure that no one knows that you were brought from this house. Nor will anyone other than me know your name. They only know you as Ghost Walker. All right?"

"Yes. All right. Will you do me one favor? Will you

please be as careful as you can be out there with me? I love you, Gunner. I don't want anything to happen to you. Your mom would kick both our asses." Gunner laughed. Chandler didn't hear him do that often and was glad that his brother still knew how to do it. "I'll see you in the morning. Do I want to know what is going to happen to Mr. Gauthier?"

"No, you don't." Nodding, Gunner left them after kissing Pip on the cheek and handing her to him. Chandler didn't say anything, as Sasha seemed to be processing what she'd just been asked to do. Or she was thinking of Gunner's answers to her question.

"What did he do in the service? Do you know?" He told her that he didn't. "I'm sure that it's going to take a woman to get it out of him. If she can't, then no one will. But he looks haunted to me. Like...I don't know. Like he's ready to die and thinks no one would care if he did."

"You really don't think he's thinking that, do you?" She shrugged and told him that Gunner had a lot of ghosts with him. "What sort of ghosts? Ones that you think will hurt him in some way?"

"No. I think they were people that he helped but didn't make it. They don't want to talk to me so much as they wish to speak to him. You didn't see them?" Chandler told her that he'd not seen anyone. "Strange. I don't know, Chandler, but I can tell you this. If he ever comes to us for help, in any way whatsoever, I think we should go well beyond what we think is safe for us and help him. If he's asking, then he does need it."

"Like today?" Sasha said that today, she thought, was a test. That he was figuring out who would help him or not. "I don't want him to test us. I want him to come to me when he needs me. I need him so much more than he needs me."

"Then tell him." Nodding at her when she left with Pip, Chandler thought about what Sasha had said, telling Gunner that they needed him. Also, he'd bet that he needed to hear that they loved him. Chandler did too. More than he could have anyone in the world, with the possible exception of his new family, he loved all his brothers.

Concentrating on a class schedule was a little more difficult now. He wanted to call his brother and ask him if what Sasha said was true. But deep in his heart, he didn't want to know either.

Gunner had been gone most, if not all, of his adult life. When he'd only been seventeen, he'd signed up to go into the army. Dad and Mom both were against it, but since that was what he wanted to do, they'd both signed the paperwork to give Gunner to the army to care for. That was the way his mom had put it too. That they were going to care for him now.

About a week later, Chandler had been sent home from school because he'd passed all the tests that were needed for his grade group. Coming home, he'd caught his mom at the table sobbing. Her face was red, and her nose was running. When he asked her what was wrong, she told him that she'd heard from Gunner. Nothing more than that, just that she'd heard from him. Chandler wanted to reach out to his brother and ask him what the hell he had done to their mom when Sawyer had found him instead.

"He didn't hurt her." Chandler asked his older brother why she was crying then. "She misses him. Nothing more than that. And when he wrote to her, telling her how much he missed us as well, it hurt her heart that he wasn't here for her to give him a hug. I think we forget, as teenagers, that adults need hugs too. Don't you think?"

He'd never once thought about hugging his parents after he'd turned fourteen. Now there he was, all those years later, wanting one bad enough for him to race his brother down the stairs to get one from their mom. After that, Chandler had hugged his parents every chance he got. He realized now that he should have been hugging his brothers as well, not just when he saw them and when he left.

Chandler knew there were times when he'd been growing up that a hug would have been nice. Even now, he thought that a big bear of a hug would have made him feel much better about himself. Not just today, but there were times when he'd seek out someone to greet them for a hug. That, he just realized, was just plain stupid.

Resolving to hug his family more often, he dug into the paperwork again. There was just too much for one person to go over alone. Getting up, stretching himself, he decided to go and find his mate. It was time for the two of them to break in their new bed that had arrived an hour ago.

She was just putting Pip in her bed when he came up behind her. She was warm and soft, and he loved holding her. When he started to nibble on her ear, her laughter had him harder than he'd expected. It was sexy and soft, so much like Sasha's body was.

"I did wonder how long it was going to take us to make sure that the bed was perfect. Actually, I could care less if it's perfect. I just want to have you inside of me." He hissed while he rolled his hips into her bottom so she could feel what she did to him. "Chandler, I've been waiting for what seems like years for you to take me. So unless you want me to come right now and wake Pip, you'd better take me someplace where we can scream."

The baby had been moved to her own room yesterday. Sasha and himself had been awakened every what seemed like thirty seconds while they'd made do with an air mattress. Neither of them had gotten a good night's sleep while Pip slept through the night, not waking once. The little poop head was moved when Mom told them that they shouldn't have put her in there in the first place.

Picking Sasha up in his arms, he carried her to their room. The bed was made. Since he'd not been the one to make it, he assumed that Sasha had been anticipating them using it soon. Had he known that, he might have hunted her down earlier.

Putting her on the bed so that her legs hung on either side of him, he looked into her face as he slowly unbuttoned her blouse. There was no need for words. They had been touching each other every chance they got since they moved into this house. They had been using foreplay for days now, and both of them seemed to be ready for the real thing.

"I love you, Sasha." Chandler kissed her, making short work of not just her blouse but her bra as well. When she was topless, she leaned back on the bed so that he could remove her pants. Instead, he took one of her lovely breasts into his mouth and sucked on it hard. Her fingers in his hair were nearly his undoing. Lifting his head from her, he watched her as she undid her pants for him. "I've wanted you for so long, I cannot wait to see if your body is as beautiful as I have been thinking it is. Your breasts have surpassed my wildest expectations. I know that the rest of you will as well."

"Hurry. I need to feel you touching me, Chandler."

He took her pants off with her panties. He could only stare at what she was offering him. Not only was she the most beautiful creature that he'd ever seen, but her curls were dewy for him as well.

Wanting to taste her, he got down on his knees in front of her. Spreading her legs wider, he watched her face to see the emotions that were there. Want and need were fighting for control over her. She wanted him to touch her, but she also seemed to want to touch him just as badly.

Sliding his finger through the curls and into her, he loved it when she moaned loudly and laid all the way back on the bed. Fucking her this way, stretching and giving her as much pleasure as he could, Chandler reached down and pulled his own pants open. The cool air of the room nearly had him crying out, his cock was so painfully sensitive.

Sliding his tongue through the wet lips of her nether region, he suckled on her clit until she cried out with her first climax. When she begged him to take her, Chandler did what he had wanted since he'd sat down in front of her. He leaned into her pussy and fucked her none too gently with his tongue. Sasha screamed several times into a pillow that was near her.

Sasha squeezed his head tightly with her legs, begging him to release her so that she could feel him inside of her. He wasn't ready for that. He wanted to play. Tasting her like this, drinking down her nectar, he moaned every time she flooded his mouth with more.

Chandler fucked her with his fingers as well, stretching her pussy so that she'd not hurt when he took her. He knew his cock was larger than a human's would be. That was why he was being extra sensitive to her needs. He didn't want to cause her any discomfort the first time they made love.

"Chandler, please. I'm begging you to take me. I need to feel you inside of me more than I need to breathe." He sat up when she yanked his head up by his hair. Even his cat was afraid of her at that moment. "Fuck me."

He stood up, pulling his pants off the rest of the way. Not waiting for her to tense up again, Chandler filled her with his cock. He didn't know which of them had suffered more from the abrupt invasion, her or him. His cock was strangled within her. Twisted up like it was, he couldn't move. As soon as her hips moved, adjusting herself, he guessed, to take him, he moved too. It was both painful and pleasant at the same time.

Taking her mouth with his, he kissed her as he took her, touching her body with his hands everywhere he could reach. Her ankles tightened around him when he lifted her ass up to meet his downward demands. Each time she cried out for more, his body seemed to understand that she meant it. His heart, still careful, didn't want her to hurt after they were done.

"Give yourself to me."

Her command was like a smack to his back. He nearly screamed out his own release when she bowed up from the bed, calling out his name over and over as she released. His back felt the rawness as she raked her fingers down over him. Blood, hot, raced down his back, and he could feel it gather on his spine.

When she came a second, then a third time, Chandler joined her. He came so many times that he told her he couldn't move again, he was dizzy with it. Rolling to his back, taking her with him, Chandler moved so that he was still inside of her, fucking her slowly so that her continued climaxes had a little more punch to them than she would have had without him.

Closing his eyes from the way the room swayed around, he held tightly to Sasha until he could see better. It helped that he knew better than to look with both eyes at the same time. Just looking out one eye was enough to make him ill to his stomach.

~*~

"Are you all right?" Chandler grunted at her. "Chandler, did I kill you or not? Please answer me."

"I do believe that I am dead. You killed me when

all I wanted to do was make love to my pretty little unsuspecting mate. Who knew you had this inner demon in you that was a wild cat." He looked at her with one eye. "You, my dear, are nearly too much for my poor body."

Sasha laughed and sat up over him. She could feel his cock there, semi hard and still deep within her. When he put his hands on her hips, rolling herself over him seemed to be what he wanted. Christ, it had her crying out in delicious delight when he rolled his hips up to meet hers.

"You keep that up, and we'll both be dead. They'll find our bodies connected in the most intimate way, and they'll wonder what we've been up to." Chandler laughed when she did. "You are far and away the most fun I've ever had in bed before. Including my BOB."

"You have a battery operated boyfriend? Christ, woman, you should have said something like that before. Do you still have it?" She said that no, sadly, she'd lost it on one of her moves. "We'll get you another one. I've never used one before, but I've heard that it's a lot of fun."

"Never used one before, huh? Pull the other leg, Chandler Bishop. That one is long enough, thank you." She tisked at him. "Don't lie to me. If you have used one before, just tell me if you really enjoyed it. I do not want any names."

"I swear, I haven't ever used one before."

She believed him. Of course, that didn't stop her from teasing him about it. When he rolled her to her back, making her squeal in amusement, she held his face in her hands as she kissed him several times before stretching them out to be one long, wonderful kiss.

"I love you so much." She told him that she was in love with him too. "I can hear the baby. I'll be right back."

He pulled on his jeans but didn't button them up. She'd not realized how late it was, so she got into the bed and straightened up the blankets. She could hear him talking to Pip, saying that she had the most perfect timing. He told her that he loved her for that.

When the two of them came into the bedroom, not only had she been changed, but he had a fresh bottle with him as well. Handing her to Sasha, he pulled his pants off again, pulled on his boxers, and got into bed with them.

"I was thinking while I was changing her. What are we going to tell her about her birth? I don't know if you were told this or not, but Holly pulled some strings and made it so both our names are on her birth certificate. I don't know if she did that legally or not. I didn't ask her." Sasha said that Holly had told her. "Good. So, she's a Bishop legally, and you're not. We're going to have to take care of that soon. How about tomorrow?"

"I don't know. Marry you tomorrow, or work on paperwork for the new contract that I've been given by Gunner. I'm having Holly's attorney take a look at it for me. I don't want to be caught up in anything that is going to put me on the front page of the paper again. Mom did that to me, and I don't want to have to go through that again." He laughed when she did. "You arrange it, and I'll be there. I really do need to spend more time working than I have been. It's been really distracting with all the things going on here. Not just with the new baby and a home, but just having you here too. When do you start classes?"

"I've already been taking a few. Right now, I'm working on some of the credits that I get from working with Joe." She asked him if his real name was Doctor Joe. "No, it's actually Ronald Joseph. He likes being called a shorter form of it. Since no one would call him Ronald, he started referring to himself as Doc Joe. It's stuck."

"You'll be a good vet. You seem to have a way with all kinds of animals and humans." He told her that he wanted to be a vet because he could work with the shifters as well. "Oh, I never thought of that. I mean, I can see you doing that as well. Does Doc Joe do that?"

"No. I mean, he will work with a shifter if he needs to, but he doesn't like to. I don't know why. He's not prejudiced of them or anything. He says that he's afraid of something about them. I don't know what it could be, but he is." Sasha watched Chandler when he picked up Pip and burped her. She burped like an old man. "There's my girl. Such a daddy's little trooper."

Sasha wanted to slap him, but he was just too cute right now. He was holding onto the baby like she was nothing more than a loaf of bread in his hand. Even after only a few days of having her here, they both were getting really good at not just holding her, which had scared them both to death at first, but changing her as well. Getting her buckled into a car seat was still a challenge for them, but they were getting the hang of it. The biggest challenge she'd ever had to face was putting the seat in the car in the first place.

It had taken them watching several videos on the computer to put it together. The cloth on the inside of it hadn't been put in place when they purchased it. After getting that where they thought it belonged, they had to start all over with it because it was upside down. Then they had to put the sucker in the car.

She'd never cursed so much in her life. Sasha had broken not one nail but three, cut her hand on the seatbelt lock, as well as hit her head several times on the door frame as she was trying to get it in level by the leveler that came with it.

Chandler ended up in worse shape than she had, and had taken cursing to a new level. His cat seemed to be just as frustrated as they had been. Twice he'd tried to throw the car seat in the trash, and she had only just been able to stop him. He had broken a finger and also torn his pants and shirt. Chandler made her throw them away because every time she looked at them, she'd burst out laughing.

Car seat installation was not for the faint of heart. They decided that when they got it into the car, they weren't going to show Raven or Sawyer how to install it. They were going to record every second of it and make sure that they showed it to everyone they knew. Sasha was just glad that there had been no one around when they'd been working on theirs. There was no telling how long they'd have to live with someone bringing it up.

"I've arranged everything. I don't know about you, but I'd rather just go the short route to get married. We have a daughter, and we have a home, so getting married seems to be just a tad out of order." She told him that she'd never been one of those little girls who dreamed of a big wedding. "Neither had Raven, thankfully—she has a lot of friends. Anyway, we'll get to the courthouse at noon. They're going to marry us on their lunch break so long as we provide food. I've already spoken to my mom, and she's having the food brought in from the leap ladies club. They're happy to have something to do, she told me."

"My goodness, you have been busy, haven't you? What else do you—?" She paused when she saw the ghost standing in their room. Chandler looked in the direction that she was looking and got out of bed after handing Pip to her. "Chandler, be careful."

"I will. I'd rather do this with you nearby so that I can do it correctly. Tell me what I'm supposed to do." Hailey appeared, but she stood by Chandler without saying anything. She could guide him through this, of that Sasha had no doubt. "Hailey, what's going on here?"

"He isn't sure what has happened to him." Chandler only nodded. "He knows that something has come about, but he's not sure what it is. He's been murdered. That's all I can tell you right now."

"Hello." The man looked up at him, and Sasha covered Pip's face with the blanket. He had assuredly been murdered. "What can I do for you? Do you know where you are?"

"No." Chandler asked the questions, as Hailey told him to ask them. "Do you see anything around where you came from? Are there people with you? What does the outside look like if you can see a window or a door?"

"My home. I was at my home when someone came into the room with me." Hailey had Chandler ask if he knew who it was. "My brother. He came into my bedroom like he owned the place."

Anger spilled off the man. He was remembering more of being shot three times in the head. Most of his face was missing. Sasha could see that the man had suffered badly. Thinking that the shots to the head were where the last of the bullets had entered him, she noticed that he had defensive wounds on his arms and chest. Angry ghosts were strong and unpredictable.

"I can help you if you will tell me where it is you came from." The man said that he had it now. He was going to kill his brother. "No. You do that, and you'll be sent away forever. To a place that you'll never talk, see, or interact with anyone again. Tell me where you are."

"No."

When he lashed out at Chandler, his cat took his body. The man, nothing more than a specter, screamed and fell backward. He couldn't be hurt, but in his mind, a large white tiger was leaping at him, and it scared him badly enough that he calmed down.

Chapter 7

Hanging up the phone, he looked at Sasha. She was still laughing at him, and he wanted to strangle her. He wouldn't, of course, but he still didn't think that having his boxers trapped around his legs when he shifted was all that humorous. He might have hurt himself.

"Are you finished?" She nodded, then laughed again. "I cannot wait to change you so that you can mess up, and I can have a good time at your expense."

"You should have seen it from where I was. There is this large white tiger flying through the air at a ghost. Your tiger had the legs of his boxers tangled up around his hind legs like he was wearing some kind of leggings. Then, if that wasn't funny enough, him trying to kick them free while being so cool about it nearly had me falling off the bed. I wish I had had my phone out. That would have been something to use as our family Christmas card this year." He told her that he didn't like her right now. "Yes, you do. I'm telling you right now that I will never see you shift again without having myself a little giggle. What did Sawyer say about the man?"

"He still has some contacts at the station house, and he's making sure that they're aware that it might be a homicide." Sasha asked him if the bullet holes would be a giveaway. "Yes, but you can't just say that and not have questions asked of you. They'd think.... Well, maybe not, but they might have to wonder why he knew all about it. I doubt they will because you've been working with them, but who knows. People can be very strange when shit like this happens in their house."

"I guess that is a police term. By the way, your mom is going to take care of Pip for us while we take a little time away from things around here. Also, I've sort of gotten us a few days without ghosts coming around. Hailey is spreading the word about it now." He asked her if she thought that was going to work. "I don't know. I've never asked before. However, if we have sex like we did all night last night, I might be joining the dead."

He was still smiling about what she'd said when she left him there. He was still going over class requirements and had been able to take off about sixty hours of classes on his own. When Doc Joe looked them over to assess what he'd done for him, maybe he'd have a few more hours under his belt. Even with what he had done himself and what he'd already taken, he was nearly two years finished with his six-year projected timeline.

We're at the house. The wife and the brother are gone. I don't suppose you might have heard where they are. Chandler told him that he had no idea. *I didn't think so, but that's fine. We'll find them. Also, there was a lot of paperwork lying about. And you might not have figured this out with the man talking to you, but the house was set on a timer to blow at six tonight. I believe that is why there is so much evidence lying around. They didn't figure anyone would be looking for the man until after the house blew, and all that would have gone up with the house. I'm sure that they were planning for this to happen while they were gone with a very strong alibi. I have no idea how they expected the body to have bullets in it when we found him. People are stupid – you know that, don't you?*

I have begun to realize that, yes. Are you going to be able to be at the courthouse at noon for us? Sawyer said that he'd not miss it for the world. *Molly is ready to be her bridesmaid. I heard the two of them, Sasha and her, talking this morning about what she was wearing. You have yourself a great kid there, Sawyer.*

She's amazing. Her skills are getting better daily, as well. Just last night, she showed us that she can dress herself with a thought. Who would have thought that just a drop or two of my blood would have done so much for her? Chandler said that she was alive, and that was all that mattered. *I couldn't agree more on that one.*

Also, Sawyer, I know that I've said this to you before, but I really can't thank you enough for your help with the house. With everything. The house that you helped Sasha buy that her mother lived in was nice for her. It gave her some leverage that she needed.

Her mom is going away for a very long time. She knows that, doesn't she? Chandler said that she was glad for it. *As for the house and stuff, don't sweat it, Chandler. Raven said that she wanted all her family to be safe and happy. Having a home of my own? I've never felt so secure in my life. Even growing up at home with all of us, we were never really safe there. I mean, the roof or some other disaster was just a nice strong storm from us losing it all. Mom and Dad are looking at smaller homes now. I hope they want to build something on the land. I think they'll love that better.*

They were telling me that they don't want Raven to do anything for them. That she might need her money for a rainy day. And this is what got me the hardest. They said that they don't have a lot of years left, and we shouldn't be bothering with them. I nearly sobbed when she said that to me. Sawyer said it would have hit him hard as well.

What is that supposed to mean? I mean, I know that they're getting older, but hell, they could go for another fifty years or so. I don't want to think about losing them, Sawyer. I mean, they're all we have.

I know what you mean. I'm going to have Raven talk to them. Holly too. I think she might be a little older than them, so who knows if she can talk some sense into them. If nothing else, it might make them think of the time they have left and not say that anymore. Chandler said that he didn't want them pissed off. *No. Neither do I. But I do want them to start living while they have time. I'm not going to let them sit back and wait for death to take them. That would be more heartbreaking than for them to die too soon, don't you think?*

I agree.

After asking him to let him know if he heard anything else, they closed the connection. Chandler still had about two hours before he had to head to the courthouse, and he wanted to make sure that everything that he'd gotten was in place.

After making two phone calls, he thought that while a courthouse marriage would be quicker, that didn't mean that he had to skimp on things. And this, he'd paid for on his own. The cleaning of the ring that he'd found for Sasha secondhand was done. He had flowers put in place for her and Molly to hold. Also, he'd hired the local art teacher to take some pictures of the day for them. All in all, he thought that he'd done a good job. Mostly thanks to his mom helping him.

Smiling, he was closing down his computer when a news flash came across the news app that he had. It said that there was a police chase on Route Forty that was in progress. Pulling up the feed, Chandler watched as two cruisers chased after a little sedan that looked like it was going to crash with every turn it took.

"I was thinking about—what is that you're watching?" He moved so that Sasha could watch too. "I've seen that car before. I think that's my brother's. I thought that he was in jail."

"I'll ask Sawyer. He might know about it."

When he reached out to his brother, he told him what he was watching and who he thought it might be. Sawyer told him that he'd get back with him. Ten minutes later, he was calling him on the phone. Chandler put the phone on speaker so that Sasha could hear it too.

"He was in custody as of eight this morning. They found the body of the officer in the hall of the cells and put out an all-points for him. So far, we have two dead officers and a stolen cruiser. The cruiser is still missing, as is one more officer. Female. They're worried for her safety too." Chandler asked him how he'd gotten armed. "I don't know that right now. The officer in the hallway was still armed. He was killed when Zack stabbed him in the chest with a butter knife. They're looking into how he got it now. Also, the other officer has his service weapon but not his ankle weapon. All cops—all that I worked with anyway—always have a secondary. Hang on a moment."

"Are they fearing that Zack might rape the female officer? He can't. I mean, he can't have an erection. The only reason that I know is because he had an accident about five years ago, and it caused some major damage to his groin. Not only did they have to remove one of his testicles, but a portion of the second one. He can't get it up."

Telling that to Sawyer when he came back on the line, he thanked him for the information, but he told them that not all rapes were just body to body. Chandler could see that Sasha was confused for a moment. Then when it hit her what he was saying, her face paled. He held her hand while she sat on the desk with him, still watching the camera in the sky keep up with her brother's car.

They were both listening to Sawyer tell them what else he knew about the situation. Then, just in a blink of an eye, it was done. The car that Zack was driving tried to make a left turn too sharply onto another back road when it simply went airborne. As it rolled over and over, Chandler watched as things flew out of the car as it hit another car, an electrical pole, as well as several bushes. When it came to a landing on the yard of a home that he'd driven by a hundred times, he watched with his breath held to see if anyone got out. Nothing seemed to move for what felt like hours. Then the police cruisers arrived.

"They just told me about the accident. Are you watching it still?" Chandler said that he and Sasha both were watching it. "The police just confirmed to me that he's dead. Sadly, so is the officer. She was buckled in while Zack was ejected from the car before it stopped. I'm so sorry, Sasha. My heart breaks for you."

Instead of saying anything, she left Chandler there. He told Sawyer what she'd done, and he suggested that he give her a minute. Watching this unfold was like having a bad dream. Chandler might not have ever met the younger man, but he was related to him through Sasha.

When she returned a few minutes later, she was followed by Zack himself. The man had wasted no time at all in coming for his sister to help him.

"I don't have the ability to make you alive, you fucking moron. You're dead. What the hell did you expect to happen when you escaped from jail and went on a high speed race across the state with troopers behind you? Did you think they'd just say, 'Wow, he's going really fast, let's not bother with him'? You fucking shit. You're dead, deal with it. Or not. I could care less. Now I have to go tell Mom what her precious baby boy did, and how now he's dead because he doesn't have one brain cell left. By the looks of you, I'd say that was about right. What the hell were you thinking?"

"I was thinking that I didn't want to go to fucking jail. You said you were able to talk to ghosts. Okay, I believe you now. So, since I'm your brother, you can work some of your boozy juice on me and make me alive." She asked him what boozy juice was, and Chandler had to laugh. Zack really was an idiot. "It's whatever it takes for you to make me alive. You can do it special like for me, right? I'm your brother."

"Yes, so you are. And even if I had this boozy juice, or whatever you think it is called, there is no way in hell that I'd bring you back. Want to know why?" Zack nodded. "Because you're fucking dead."

When she shouted out the last part of her statement to Zack, Chandler lost it. He was laughing too hard to hear what else was being said to Zack because he had to leave the room. Christ, he'd not laughed as hard as he had in the last few days than he thought he had in his entire adult life.

He was in the hallway when Sawyer reached out to him again. After telling him that Zack was there with them, he had him ask where the husband was of the officer that he'd killed. Going into the office again, he saw that Zack was still arguing with Sasha, who looked as if she was ignoring him. He didn't know how that was working for her—Zack was right up in her face.

"Where is the husband of the officer that was in your car when you killed yourself?" Zack said he didn't know what he was talking about. "Of course you do. You might be dead, but you have a good enough memory to know that your sister can talk to you. Where is he?"

"I don't know what you're talking about."

Chandler nearly walked away, then had a sudden thought. If they could get angry and hurt someone, why couldn't he? Letting his cat take him, Chandler lunged at the ghost and felt the impact of their anger meeting.

Chandler might have thought about this more had he more time, or had even guessed what was going to happen. Or even had a small clue of what might take place when his formed cat hit the body of a pissed off ghost.

It wasn't like he'd seen in the movies where he got all slimed up. No, it was much worse than that. Chandler saw every movement of Zack's death. The way he'd been flipped over and over in the car until he flew out the front windshield. Hitting the pavement and having his already broken body torn up from the gravel and other things that tore into him. There was no pain to what he witnessed, but he could control it. He knew too that the woman in the car with him had been dead before Zack had left the garage where she'd parked the cruiser.

Backing himself up, like one would rewind a movie, he went back further and further in the dream-like state he was in. He saw where the woman suddenly appeared in front of him and went back slowly. This was by far the strangest thing he'd ever done.

Chandler did wonder for a moment what was going on with his body. Did he look dead? Was he still his cat? Regardless, he thought to himself, he was getting information that he didn't think he'd get any other way.

The woman came out of her house, kissing her husband goodbye. Once he had knowledge of the man, he let it go ahead now. Just a frame or two at a time. The man's death, a horrid thing, had Chandler cringing from it. Zack had killed them both right there on the front stoop of the house. Chandler knew where the man's body was and how he'd murdered him.

"Chandler." He looked up at Sasha when she said his name. She asked him if he was all right, and as his cat, he realized, he told her that he was just fine. "Good. Zack disappeared as soon as you hit the floor just now. I don't know what you did, but it must have hurt him quite a bit. I've never seen anyone go through a ghost like that before. Did it hurt you?"

"No. How long was I out?" Sasha asked him what

he meant. "I must have been out for a while. I got to see, like you would on a reel to reel movie, everything that Zack did in the last few hours. I wonder if I could have seen more if I had thought about it. I could even rewind like I would a movie. It was fucking strange."

"You didn't do anything but just jump through him and land right there. Zack sort of paused as you were about halfway through him, then he exploded, like fireworks on the Fourth. What do you think might have happened?" He told her what he'd seen. "He killed them both then. I guess I knew that he had, but I didn't want to believe it. Now, what do you have to do? Besides call Sawyer."

Chandler looked up at the grandfather clock when it dinged the half-hour. They had thirty minutes to get to the courthouse. He told Sasha that he'd tell his brother then. If he didn't make it to the wedding, then he'd use their link.

Rushing around, they were thankful that the baby was going to stay there with the nanny they'd hired. His mom would come and get her after the wedding, but for now, having to figure out the car seat and the diaper bag again would have surely made them late.

They were pulling up in front of the big building just as the clock was dinging in the big clock over the courthouse. Not only was Sawyer there, but there were state police as well as cops from a few jurisdictions that he'd never heard of. But today, he didn't care. He was getting married. Whatever happened now could wait. He had his wedding to attend, and he was finished with Zack as far as he was concerned.

~*~

Sasha listened to what Chandler was saying to the officers that were there. Sawyer said that he wasn't working the case but helping out because he knew the area so well. It was a time like this that having someone know the area would not help at all. Al Windermere was not just dead, but while the police had been chasing Zack, he'd thrown out the man's body parts as he drove. Chandler had witnessed it all once he figured out what her brother had done.

"He must have known just where he was going because he not only knew where everything was in the garage to make it happen, but he also had it figured out what time Cindy left for work." One of the officers asked why he'd hit them and not one of the other twenty cops that lived closer to the station. "She was on the arresting team that was there when he was taken down. I guess he figured that he'd get some payback before he was put in prison."

"Now, he's dead." The officer shook his head as he stood there, asking questions. "What sort of person does that to another human being? I know that there are sick individuals out there, but to take a man who did nothing more than be married to a cop and do that to them? I just can't think about it too hard. It breaks my heart to have to tell that couple's parents what a horrible thing has been done to them. I have a good mind not to tell them at all. Just let them know that their son died in the execution of a crime and leave it at that. If they ask me if they need to identify him? Well, then I'll just explain to them that there is no need for that. His body was badly damaged in the accident. Not a lie, just stretching the truth a little bit."

Sasha thought that was a good way to go with breaking the news to the family. However, from what she'd seen already on the news, not only did she think that the family knew that their loved ones were dead, they had a good idea who had done it as well. She had seen her brother after he was dead and thought that seeing another man in worse shape might be more than she could handle.

Zack had made a name for himself as he went out, not just from the mutilation of the man and his wife, but the fact that he'd killed three officers as well as stolen a car. Sasha thought that if he did come back, she'd ask him about it. She even said that to Chandler.

"Don't. That's what he wants, I think. To have people talking about him. Saying his name. I think that what the captain said to Sawyer before the news media arrived about not saying his name is the best way to handle this. Don't give him anything he wants. Even dead, you know that he's out there someplace bragging about his kills and what he did to that couple. Just don't mention it at all. Honey, I'd be more worried about what you're going to tell your mother and sister."

"That he's dead and nothing more. If they want more, they can ask about it. But as far as I'm concerned, that's all I'm going to say. They had to know, both of them, that this was where he was headed. Zack has never been not in trouble. From the time—it doesn't matter now. He's gone, and it's over with." She smiled up at him. "I'm going to go do it now, I think. While the wedding is still fresh in my mind. I'm not going to let them take my good feelings away by telling them what we did, but I am going to tell them both that Zack is gone and that there will be no funeral services for him. I can't afford it anyway."

Chandler knew that any one or all of his family would pay for the funeral. They'd even have a big one should Sasha want it. But to him, this was the best way to deal with it. Have him cremated with no mention of it in the paper at all. It would be hard enough having a funeral for someone that the community would hate when they found out eventually anyway.

He went with her to the jail. One of the cops had made it so that her sister and mother were in the same room when they went to see them. The recording of the accident hadn't been released yet to the general public, and he wondered if it would be. He got permission from the captain to show it to Zack's sister and mother so that they'd know what had happened. Chandler had a feeling that they'd believe that Sasha was lying. And that just would break her heart, he thought.

"So, you've come to bail us out. I think that is only fitting since you're the one that put us in here anyway. What do you have to say for yourself, Sasha? I'm sure that you should begin by saying how sorry you are that you got us into trouble." Sasha told them that they'd done the trouble all on their own. "And we would have kept right on doing well for ourselves if you'd just kept your fucking nose out of our shit. You even made your sister cry. They embarrassed her when they told her that she'd have to have a reinforced cot. Not to mention bigger blankets. You're nothing but a fucking whore. That's all you are. A whore that should have been strangled at birth."

"I worked really hard to lose all that weight too, and they just had to make fun of me like I didn't slim down a great deal. You're just a bitch. You always have been jealous of my being able to shed the pounds when you had to work so hard at it." Sasha rolled her eyes at her sister when she started wailing about how she'd lost hundreds of pounds, and now she was in here. "They said that I'd have to go on a program and lose more weight. How the hell am I going to lose anything, Sasha? I'm going to waste away to nothing because of you."

"Oh, fucking stop lying to yourself. You've not lost a single pound, Pearl. You're fat, get over yourself. And you'll be fat until someone starts giving you only food that is good for you. You've not lost hundreds of pounds. It would take years—no, decades—for you to waste away to nothing. Holy Christ, you both drive me insane." She looked at her mother. "You have no right to say those things to me. None at all. I've not given you a single reason to blame me for whatever shit you've gotten yourself into."

Chandler wanted to tell her family for her. He'd told her that all the way here. When she turned to him now, he could see the pleading in her eyes, begging him to do what she just couldn't.

When she turned and left him there to do this, Chandler drew in a deep breath. Just tell them, his mind screamed at him. But his heart thought that he could do it calmer. However, when Katie told him to shit or get off the pot, his heart simply froze up for them.

"Zack is dead. He killed three officers this morning, as well as a civilian. After taking off in a patrol car right after he killed the first officer, he went to the Windermere's home and killed them both." Katie told him he was a liar. "Believe what you will, but he's dead. He would have been executed by the state for his actions today anyway, so this will save the state some money on having to house and take care of the idiot. Yes, he was an idiot. Who in the world thinks that they can outrun the police after murdering one of their brothers? No one. And if you call my wife a whore again, I will hunt you down and make what happened to your son look like you're trying out for the beauty pageant. And you—" He looked at Pearl. "Grow the fuck up and look at yourself in the mirror. The only person shoving food in your face is yourself. Zack is dead. Blame that on yourself if you want to. But never my wife again."

He let his cat take him, not caring at all that he was in his only good suit, or that there were cameras rolling all around him, and several officers nearby. He snapped at them both, letting them see the large and dangerous teeth that he had. Then when he thought they had screamed enough about what he'd done, he lifted his leg up and pissed on both of them. Not just on their feet, but all the way up to their laps. Fucking bitches needed to be taught more of a lesson, but he wanted to go on his short honeymoon. With his wife. Hell, he might not even read a single paper when he was gone.

Walking out of the station, he heard someone

applauding. Pausing long enough to look around, there were more people doing the same thing. Not just officers, but there were undercover cops, as well as his wife and family. They were cheering him on for what he'd said to the other two, but also how he'd handled pissing on them.

Immature? Yes, yes, it was. But he didn't regret it at all. He might not ever do anything like that again, but he sure was feeling pretty good about himself for doing it today. Until he looked at his mom. She stood there, tapping her foot at him.

"Did you enjoy that?" He nodded at her, putting his forehead on her knee to show her how sorry he was. "Well, I did not. I wanted to piss on them too. To call my daughter a whore? Well, if they do it again, I'm going to be the one peeing on them. You got that, Chandler?"

Yes, ma'am. He looked up at her. *You cursed. I don't think I've never heard you curse before in all my life.*

"I'm about as mad as I've ever been before." He told her that he'd been that way too. "Good. I love you to pieces, Chandler, but you need to do that more often. You're the softest one of my sons, not a girly soft, but you have a tender heart. Don't let those people railroad you into feeling sorry for them. You keep on showing that you're a tiger and not a man who wouldn't hurt a fly. All right?"

I can do that.

She scratched him behind the ear before turning her back to him. When she told someone to go out to their car and get him something to put on, all five of his brothers and his dad took off running. Chandler thought that they were just as shocked as he was about hearing their mom curse. It was going to be marked on his calendar when he got home. He might, someday, make it a special holiday or something on his own personal calendar. He'd have to give that some thought.

He changed into some jeans and a T-shirt before leaving the courthouse. When a limo pulled up in front of the steps where they were standing, he kissed Sasha and told her that he loved her. After getting into the car and it driving away, she turned to him.

"I love you, Chandler. Thank you for today. It was beautiful. All the flowers and the cake. The pictures were a nice touch too." He told her that he loved her, as well. "I have an idea. Let's head to the hotel and have some fun, then tomorrow let's go get Pip and take a long drive to Amish country. I've not been there in ages. It'll be a nice way for us to forget about all the shit that is going on."

"Excellent idea, my dear. Excellent. We'll have to get some things while there. I know that my mom loves to get some of their cheeses and such. Dad will murder us if we don't bring him back some jerky."

Sasha giggled. "I love you more with each beat of my heart, Sasha Bishop."

"And I love you more than that, Chandler Bishop."

They were both laughing all the way to the hotel. He had plans for his little bride after he fortified himself with a nice thick steak with all the trimmings. His parents had gotten him a gift card, and he planned to use it all tonight with Sasha.

Chapter 8

Gunner had brought Sasha out the morning that he'd told her he would, and now he was digging up places that he had marked himself. There were forty graves out here—not graves, he supposed, but plots of ground that held the dead. The saying that the dead didn't tell you much, or something like that, wasn't true. They were telling them plenty today. Sasha had contacted a couple of the ghosts so that they'd be prepared to be dug up today.

"Why did you have to tell them?" Sasha just looked at him, a look of confusion on her face. "The dead. Why did you warn them that they'd be found today? I'm sure that there is a good reason. No one has to know it, but I am curious."

"Most of these dead have been in the ground for a great many years. I wanted to make sure that they were all dug up before we left. So I contacted a couple of the younger ones that I knew had been put here and asked them to let the others know. That way, if they want, they can be ready to move on if they wish it. A great many of the people out here have hung around only because they wanted their bodies to be accounted for. I guess they wanted to make sure that Gauthier got what he deserved." Gunner asked her if she thought he would. "If not from the police, then he will get it when he passes from this world to the other. They aren't to harm the living, the dead aren't. But they can take care that whoever killed them—and it must be murder—they get their piece of him. And by that, I mean they do get their piece of him. It's brutal, Hailey told me."

Gunner watched the sun coming up over the trees and wondered what the dead would do to him. He'd not been a good person at all, much less kind to the deceased. Gunner wasn't known to be kind to himself. But with this, he hoped that it might help someone that had a loved one lost here.

"Not all the dead are from Gauthier. Did you know that?" Gunner told Sasha that he'd had a feeling that he'd opened up his land for others to bury people there. "I don't know if it can help you or not, but they know who it was that killed them. I can give you that information if you want it. Also, you should know that there are more bodies than these. There are a lot of others under the sunporch that was put on twenty years ago. You'll need to get that dug up as well."

"Yes, that will be helpful. When you find out a name, all you need to do is log it in here if it's not on the list of missing people. The list is fairly long, I'm sorry. It's from about nineteen twenty until recently. None of us think that he did all this on his own, so it's good to know that he had some help with the amount out here."

Gunner watched Sasha as she spoke to nothing that he could see. When she laughed, he had to smile.

Sasha thought that she was like Raven. No one was like Raven. She'd made herself into what she was with hard work and money. Sasha had learned how to be a bitch by being street smart. She wasn't a woman that people would think they should be afraid of. Sasha was more of a "Holy shit; did you see that?" sort of woman. A slick not-in-your-face sort of get-your-ass-caught person.

"There is a man here that says that he knows where there are several young men that have been killed. They're not wanting to be found with the police here." He didn't see the other man, but he had an idea what Sasha was trying hard to say without embarrassing either of them. "He wants to know if he tells you where they are, could we please keep their names out of the paper. He said that they'd tell us if they wanted their parents notified or not."

"They're not homosexuals, I take it." Sasha said they were not. "We had a small clue that Gauthier was a sexual deviant. Is that one of the reasons that they don't want the police around?"

"No, he said. It's because they have families, children, and they don't want them to find out what they were forced to do." Gunner asked Sasha if she had an issue with them not being called out in the paper. "None at all. What happened to them was no fault of their own. There is no reason to bring up something that is neither relevant to your case or the way that I can speak to them. They were killed by this man, and that's all the newspaper or anyone else needs to know."

"Thank you." He heard the voice thanking him and looked at Sasha. She smiled at him and told him that she would head over there now to get their names and what they wanted to be done. She turned back to him before she was very far away.

"Chandler could come here and help. I think he is expecting someone to ask him." Gunner asked her if he was good enough to get with the dead. "As good as I am. And he's not as afraid of them as I can be. He's getting a name for himself with the dead that he's not to be fucked with. You might want to remember that if someone else comes around to see you."

Twenty minutes later, Chandler was coming up

from his end of the property. It was within walking distance, he knew, but he'd not realized how close. Chandler was in dark clothing like he was, and he'd even brought a clipboard and pen with him. Gunner hugged him tightly before letting him go.

"You all right?" Gunner looked away as he nodded. "You can tell me if you want. I'd never tell anyone. Not even Sasha if you didn't want her to know."

"I'm going to hell. I'll miss you there." Chandler asked him what the hell he was talking about. "Nothing. You just take the names, and we'll talk later. It's something that I've been meaning...I'm lonely, Chandler. Not for family. You guys are staying away just as much as I like it. But I don't have anyone to talk to. No friends that I can call on to shoot the shit with. All the people I know have had it as bad, if not worse than I have. I just need someone that I can, I guess you could say, depend on to be there for me. Like Sasha and Raven are for you guys."

"Sasha would murder you where you stand if she heard you saying that about her. That she's not there for you. Man, I'm not kidding, either. She loves you, Gunner." He said that he loved her as well. "If you can't talk to me about shit, then she is the one that I'd talk to. And I have a feeling that you'll have your mate coming around soon enough. That'll be a great load off your shoulders."

"A mate would go screaming into the night if they were to listen to some of the things I've done. Not to mention, I have nightmares that would give your nightmares bad dreams." Chandler said he was sorry. "Me too. You help me out with this, and we'll get out of here sooner. By the way, thank you so much for the jerky and cheese. That was just the ticket for me. I love it."

"Sasha said you'd not like it hot. I had it in my head that you'd want your cheese hotter than hell. But she said that you'd like it mild, on a cracker that has no herbs or flavors with it. She said that you'd eat it on a regular cracker if you had those." He just grinned at his brother. "Christ, she knows you better than I do. I'm telling you right now when the holidays come around, you should expect the most perfect gift from us. She got everyone's cheeses right. Even Mom and Dad. Who would have thought they'd be thrilled to death with five huge rounds of cheese that would feed an army? And Mom likes jerky, not Dad. I hadn't any idea."

Gunner laughed with his brother all morning as he took names. Wandering to where Sasha was off and on, he made sure that she was all right too. It was a little disconcerting to see her standing there, talking and nodding her head as she wrote on her own paperwork.

Just after lunch, Gauthier was served. He was

fired up about them trespassing and that they were ruining his fields when the FBI came around and took his statement. The man didn't say another word until his attorney showed up. After that, there were a lot of men and women that Gauthier worked with and for that were arrested as well when they tried to flee the country. The police and the Feds were having a very good day, Gunner thought.

"Gunner!"

He turned and drew his gun at the same time when he heard Sasha scream his name. He did notice that most of the force that he had with him had done the same thing. When Sasha came running toward him and Chandler, he saw the man chasing her at the same time. From the look on his face, he had no idea that she was leading him right to his death. Shoving her behind him and to the ground, he took out the man chasing her with his own weapon out before he could fire at them.

He didn't kill the man, mores the pity, Gunner thought. But he did wound him enough that he'd not be getting up and moving again. His knee was gone. The way he was bleeding made him think that he wasn't going to make it for much longer unless Gunner called in some help.

Nodding to the medic that was with him, Gunner made his way to the man. Kicking away his gun so that he'd not use it on them, Gunner stood over the man while the doc worked on him. He waited just long enough for the man to accuse him of shooting him for no reason.

"My sister over there, when she yells at me to do something like that, I fire first then ask questions later. What did you do to her? I know for a fact that she was armed too." Sasha came to stand with him. "I was just asking what he did to you that had you running away in fear without your weapon out."

"The fucking bastard hit me from behind and took it. He killed the man with me too by breaking his neck like he was nothing more than a twig." Sasha kicked the man on the ground in the ribs. Gunner didn't even bother holding her back. "I thought when I stood up and hit him in the head with the log that he'd just run off. But he came after me. I thought this would be the perfect place for him to come. He killed my sister Melinda and tried to murder Pip."

"You did that? I love Pip. She's such a cutie." Again the man said he didn't know what they were talking about. "Sure you do. Melinda told us who you were right before she died. If you're going to murder someone and their child, it's always a good thing to make sure that they're both dead before you run off. Not that you're going to get the chance again, you see. Right now, I have you on all kinds of charges that are going to get you killed."

"You should know too that before Melinda died, she told us how you'd been stalking her for days. That you murdered the man that was the baby's father. Even after he told you that Melinda didn't speak to the ghosts and that you had the wrong woman. She left me a list of the bodies that belong to you out here." Gunner just let Sasha talk. "She told me that your name is Charles Hockings. And that you murdered six people thinking that they were someone that spoke to ghosts."

He knew for a fact that Melinda hadn't told her anything other than that the first name of the man that killed her started with a C. Melinda had also been able to talk to the dead. Gunner was also happy that Sasha had not mentioned that she had spoken to her dead sister, only that they'd spoken. He thought that he and Sasha would make a good team if he ever worked with a partner. She was kinda cute too, like Pip.

When Hockings was arrested then put into an ambulance, Sasha looked at him before running to the nearest tree and losing her lunch behind it. Chandler came to stand with him while they waited on her, and Chandler told him, thanks. Gunner asked him for what.

"I think she was waiting for you to call her a liar. For all the things that she said to Hockings." Gunner said what he'd just been thinking about her. "She's brave when she needs to be, but as soon as it's over, she's sick like this. I think it's the stress."

"Sasha doesn't have stress, Chandler, she has smarts. Do you have any idea what would have happened to her should she had told him that she sees ghosts too? Everyone that he encountered would think he was crazy, sure, except the ones that have bodies out here, or someplace else, who wouldn't have taken the chance on her talking. Her doing what she did more than likely saved her life and yours. Because you will kill anyone that comes within a yard of her with intentions of harming her." Chandler asked him why she was ill then. "That is pent up anger. I've seen seasoned men take out an entire group of men without pausing a beat. Sometimes their death wouldn't be easy either. But after it was over, they'd have all this rushing through them and would have to get rid of it before it harmed them. Sasha is one of the strongest women I've ever had the pleasure of working with. And that would include Raven."

Handing a flask full of bourbon to Sasha to rinse her mouth out, he laughed when she coughed several times after taking a drink. Gathering up the men to take care of the other officer, they were finishing up with the last of the ambulances pulled in to carry the dead away when he called it a day for Chandler and Sasha. They had more than done what he'd asked of them, and he was going to owe them for a long time.

Not that they'd see it that way, but he'd do something for them soon.

Going to his new home, he was glad for the progress that was being made on it. They only had the main floor to do, and the entire house had been cleaned and scrubbed, the furniture removed that he didn't want, and all the walls had been painted a very bright white. He loved the cleanness of it when he walked down the halls and into rooms.

While he'd had a very good day with what he'd been doing, he also thought it was one of the more stressful days that he'd had in a while. Stripping down to his bare skin, he made his way out to the covered deck. Letting his cat take him, he ran like the hounds of hell were after him for as long as he had the breath to do it before lying down under one of the larger trees. He was nearly asleep when a deer walked by him with his herd.

This would be the third night in a row that Gunner had slept outside of his house. He knew that it wouldn't be long before it would be too cold for this. But he was enjoying the peace of the woods. There were no guns firing. No one was screaming at him to go away. Nothing was going on out here that he didn't create for himself. Even putting out the salt licks for the deer had been by design, so he could watch them as they made themselves at home. Never to kill them—just for no other reason than they were there.

Gunner knew that his coat would keep him warm and dry if it started to rain. The house wasn't that far away where he'd not be able to go there for shelter if it got really bad. Watching the little fawns that were playing around like they had not a care in the world, he thought about a mate.

Having a mate for him would be problematic. He was not just a loner, but he was a man who had demons. Some haunted him when he was quiet—others gave him nightmares at any time of the day or night. Even if he wasn't asleep, they'd come out to remind him what a terrible person he was. Smiling, he knew that if Sasha heard him say that, she'd bonk him on the back of the head. Gunner did finally close his eyes when the sun was coming up over the trees again.

~*~

Merriam was seated in her usual place—the first seat next to the dais so the judge could see her when she asked a question. She thought for sure that he'd not been able to see her those first few days she'd been in the courtroom after they'd started this waste of her tax money.

"Ms. Stipple, we're going to be doing things a little—" She cut him off and told him that she was Mrs. Addington. "No. You're not. We've established already that you cannot be legally married to Roger Addington because you weren't Merriam when you signed the marriage license. Therefore, you are forever known to everyone as Janet Stipple. We've all gone over this with you repeatedly. You were never Merriam Addington."

"You can't just erase all the years that I worked and worked for the Addington name to mean something. I demand that you stop this nonsense right this minute, and you call me by the right name. Or so help me, I will rain a world of hurt down on you that will make the last war look like a simple schoolyard fight."

The gavel came down hard and fast. It made her jump in her seat each time he hit it against the disk he had up there. When he stood up, leaning over the oak dais he was behind, she felt her spine stiffen while her anger surged up to meet his.

"Now you listen here. I'm in charge here, and I will say what is what. You sit your skinny little butt down and shut up, or so help me, you'll be the one thinking about what sort of crap storm you unleashed." She started to open her mouth. "Don't you dare. Don't you dare even think about saying another word, or I'll have you removed from here, and you'll have not one idea what fate awaits you until you read about it in the papers."

She believed him. Not that she cared, but she did want to stay and see if any of her friends would come in today to give her their support. Merriam was sure that Raven or even Holly had made sure that it wasn't in the paper for that very reason. When people cheered her on for something, Merriam shone. But not lately.

There were all sorts of things being done to her that Merriam couldn't figure out. Yesterday she'd met with an attorney that said that he was there with Roger. She'd only had to hear that Roger was sending her help, and she'd jumped right on that meeting with him.

It turned out that the attorney was there to tell her that since she'd never been Merriam Cartel, then she wasn't Merriam Addington either. Never had been. But when he mentioned that her daughter was only an Addington because Roger's name was on her birth certificate, Merriam had thrown what could only be called a hissy fit. She didn't think a brawl was what it had been, as the police were saying.

Yes, there had been a couple of chairs broken. And she had broken the man's laptop, but it had been his fault. He'd just told her that her daughter wasn't legitimate. That she'd been born without the benefit of marriage. Merriam was the greatest Addington ever born, and that she had given birth to a bastard daughter had made her see nothing but anger.

Then, not an hour later, she was called out again, this time unable to refuse any more visitors that would tell her bad news. This time it was a woman that came in to tell her that she was there to change her name on all the things that were in the name of Merriam Cartel to Janet Stipple. Thusly, all the things would then be changed from Merriam Addington, which she wasn't, to Jane Stipple.

"I'm not changing my last name to that horrid name. I changed it so that I'd be something. And I am. I am Merriam Addington, and I will not give that up because you say so." The woman, she couldn't remember her name right now, told her that a judge had said so. "I don't care what he says either. You leave my name alone. You call my husband up and tell him that I'm upset with all this. There isn't any reason for him to be doing this. Because as soon as I get out of here, I'm going to go right back to the way things were before."

"Yeah? Well, good luck with that. You have nothing left to go back to from what I've heard. The house you were living in is sold. The furniture, for the most part, has been either given away or is with the new owner. There is no place at all where your alias is now printed." Merriam asked her what that meant. "Oh, you weren't told. Well, your name is no longer Merriam Addington, so your daughter's birth certificate has been changed. The alias that was on the marriage certificate that you forged has been destroyed and stripped from the books. Also, your husband said that I was to make sure you knew that the club that you were arrested in says that they've pulled down your picture from all walls. All the clubs that you were a part of have disbanded and renamed themselves. It seems like no one wants to be associated with you or your fake names at all."

"That cannot be right. I'm a member of that place in good standing. I've never missed a day where I didn't go there to have lunch or to serve on some board. You tell them that as an Addington, I will not allow them to just dismiss me as if I wasn't anything to that place. It only exists because of me and my name." The woman just stared at her. "Write that down. I know your type. You're such an airhead that the moment that I tell you something, it goes in one ear and out the other. Write it down now, damn it. Or do I have to teach you a lesson in manners too? I will, by God. You'll see what my name can do for you. Bad or good, it's me that makes the rules."

"You think so, do you?" Merriam nodded and watched the woman get up, gathering up all her things as she spoke again. "You think you make the rules, yet here you are with your wrists and ankles chained to the table and floor. I have a dog at home that has more freedom than you do. And you teaching me manners is a joke as well. You are far and away the rudest person that I've ever come across. You think just because you have a name that you stole—yes stole—from someone that could have loved Roger that you should rule the world. I have news for you, Janet Stipple—you're nothing but a bully. A bully that preys on others to do her bidding as you sit back and think that the world owes you. No one owes you anything. Not me, not Roger, and certainly not anyone that you feel is beneath you. Which, after speaking to you for the last twenty minutes, I've figured out is everyone in the world. Christ, you're a joke. A bully and a joke."

Thinking about the little twit, Merriam had missed a great deal going on around her in the courtroom. There was a large screen in front of her seat so that she couldn't see anything or anyone that was directly in her line of vision. She could see the jurors, all thirteen of their nasty fat faces staring at her all the time, but not the judge or anyone that might be seated in the big chair next to him. Her attorney, some court appointed little prick that she couldn't fire, was seated next to her.

"What are they doing here? Why is there this monstrosity in front of me? How can I see who is talking over there?" He told her to keep her voice down. "I will not. I want to know what sort of stupidity this is. Tell me, or find someone that can answer me if you can't get your shit together enough to do that."

That was when she heard a voice on the other side of the screen. Cocking her head so that she could hear it better, making sure that she was correct—though how, she thought, could she be wrong on something like this?—she knew that her husband was over there, and he was saying the most monstrous things about her.

"Roger Addington, you shut your trap right now. I will not have you airing our private matters to anyone that comes around. Did you hear me? I said to shut up." He didn't answer her, which startled her. He never didn't answer her. "Roger? What are you doing here, anyway? I don't remember you clearing it with me to come here today. You'll leave right now and then come to see me later. Or better yet, you'll get me out of this situation that you've put me in, and I might allow you to visit that bastard daughter of Raven's. She still has it, doesn't she? I'm going to take care of that as well when you—are you listening to me, Roger?"

"We're all listening to you, Janet. Everyone in here can hear you screeching at the top of your lungs about shit that doesn't concern you." In as hard a voice as she could muster, she told him that she was his wife, Merriam Addington. "No. You were never my wife. You weren't even a good lover to me. You're a mean, cruel person that is finally getting your just desserts."

She stood up as far as she could and told him to get his lying ass to her right now. When one of the screens was moved, she looked at the man sitting in the chair next to the judge. Merriam didn't know who he was.

There as a slight resemblance to her husband, but she didn't have any idea who he was.

"It's me, Janet. Roger." She could hear him there, but it wasn't until he smiled that she recognized him. "I've not felt this good in years. Decades. I'm walking around the neighborhood again. Playing in the yard with Molly. I've even managed to lose a few pounds while I was at it."

"You look terrible. Too much sun, and look at your hair. When was the last time you had it groomed? I'm betting since I've not been home. I'll just add that to my list while I'm at it. You're much too old to be running around with your hair that long." She shook her head at him. "Roger, you will stop hanging around with that little bastard too. Also, don't be parading around the neighborhood like you're nothing but a commoner. I swear to Christ, if you didn't have me around you would have—"

"I'd have been a better father and grandfather. A better man to the people who worked for me. I would have been happier. I know for a fact that I would have had a great many more children. Children like you disposed of like they were nothing but an inconvenience." She told him that they would have been. She knew what was best for him. "You don't know shit about me, Janet. You only know things that you told me to think, to do, and to wear. I'm a new man, a better man, and you're never getting into my life again. Not ever."

"Don't be ridiculous. You were nothing before I turned you into an Addington, a name that means something." No one moved or said a word. It took Merriam a few seconds to realize what she'd said. But instead of owning the fact that she'd messed up, she lifted her chin and stared Roger right in the face. "Yes, I said that. You were doing nothing to my name when I married you. Had I not been able to trick you into marrying me, you'd still be nothing. That mother of yours and your daughter with her little bastard shouldn't have been kept alive. Raven. What a low life name. You just had to do that, didn't you, Roger? Name her after some blackbird that scavenges for food. Just as you were doing before I gave you a life worthy of the name Addington."

When Roger stood up, he stood in front of her, his body lean looking, like a much younger man who had nothing more to do than to lift weights. His laughter was different, as well. Instead of sounding forced, as she'd always heard from him, his laughter sounded like he was jolly. As if he meant to sound like he was enjoying himself. Even his face looked younger. The tan or whatever he'd been doing to himself made him almost sparkle with health. When he continued to laugh, Merriam opened her mouth to tell him to stop braying like some jackass and get to the point. But he spoke before she could.

"You're not worth it. Not one minute more of my life will be wasted on you or whatever it is you're thinking. Janet Stipple, or whatever you're calling yourself now, you can rot in hell for all I care about you. I will never think of you again after I leave here today."

Then he did just that—he left. Even with her screaming at him to get back, that she wasn't finished with him yet.

She looked at the judge, who was staring at her with his mouth open. Merriam sat down, trying her best to look like nothing Roger had said to her made a difference. It didn't, not really. She'd take him to task about this when she was home. Right now, she would do damage control on how he'd been shameless by leaving her here to deal with it on her own.

"He just doesn't understand what is going on around here. I'll have to straighten him out when I return home. And I will, too, see if I don't." She looked at the jurors, another waste of her tax money, and glared hard at them. "I'll find out where you live if I don't make it home. You just remember that. I'm not opposed to killing off each and every one of you. You just remember that when you're back there deliberating."

"What did you just say to them?" Merriam told

Judge Henry that it was none of his concern. It was between her and the people sitting together. "You just threatened an entire jury. Do you have any idea what the penalty is for that in the state of Ohio?"

"What do I care what the penalty is? I won't have to do it if they know what's good for them. Will I? But it's not a threat at all, just so you're clear on that." He said that she'd implied that it was, by voice and by look. "You misunderstand, as most people do about me. I'm not threatening them at all. I will do it if they find me anything but free to go home. The same goes for anyone in this room with me today."

"Bailiff, I want you to call the Feds in here. Ms. Stipple is going to be charged with…." Merriam watched him count everyone in the room twice before he spoke again. "Twenty-six felony counts of intimidation of a jury. Also, twenty-six misdemeanor counts of aggravated menacing, and one count of threatening a sitting state judge. I'm sure that before they get here, we can add on a few more things."

As soon as she was unchained, Merriam hit two of the officers. On one of them, she bloodied their nose, while the other one she thought she broke his leg. Jumping up and down on it, Merriam heard it snap. The jury, where she'd been headed when she'd been knocked to the floor, was scrambling like cockroaches when the lights come on. Damn it to hell.

Merriam thought that if she could just hurt one of them, it would show the others she meant business. All she got for her efforts was a bloodied mouth herself, and her entire body twisted up in a knot so that they could carry her out.

"I'll get you all. You just remember what happened here today and know that I'm not a fool like this bunch is. I'll get each of you." She thought that she heard someone saying that she was resisting arrest as well, but she didn't care. She wanted blood from these fuckers now.

She was tied up in a large rug or something when she got out to the van they'd been driving her around in. After that, they actually chained her to the floor like she was some sort of animal. Then, of all things that had been done to her, someone actually put a piece of tape over her mouth so that she wasn't able to speak. They were going to pay for this. Merriam was going to make sure that every single one of them paid big time for this shit.

Chapter 9

Raven was still laughing every time she thought of her mother being hogtied and taken away in the van. She wished that she'd been able to see it in person, but the recording of it had hit the Internet and had, in only four hours, been viewed over seven million times. Her mother was an Internet sensation. It was just too funny to think that her prim and proper mother had stooped so low.

"I guess from the look on your face that you've seen it." She nodded at Sasha. "I'm so glad that there was sound to it, aren't you? I thought hearing her tell the judge to fuck off three times as they were dragging her out of the courtroom was about as funny as anything that I've ever seen. Has your mother always been that mean?"

"Worse. The fact that she thinks she should get

away with threatening people is what I find so like her. She told one of the officers when she got back to the jail, and they took the tape off her mouth that she wanted the names of everyone that worked in the system." Sasha said she bet that went over well. "Yes, but he played right along with her. He asked her if she wanted them by dates worked or did she want them in alphabetized order. She told him both. Like she thought he was actually going to get the names for her. If I didn't know for a fact that she'd been tested for her competence, I'd swear that she was off her rocker. To think that...well, she's always thought that of herself. That she was so much better than commoners, like you and I, and that rules have never applied to her."

When Sasha sat down with her, Raven noticed something she'd not seen before. There was a mark on Sasha's neck that looked like a bruise. Standing up, she pulled her hair back and was surprised to see that it looked like a tat. A fresh one too.

"Is this something that we're all getting? I have to tell you, I'm not too terribly big on pain. Unless I'm applying it to someone else." Sasha said that it wasn't a tat. "Well, it's not a bruise, like I thought it was. What's going on?"

"I'm being marked. Both of us are. Chandler has this beautiful set of wings on his chest. They just appeared this morning, and his is complete. Mine is almost that way, but I can't see it." Raven asked her what hers was. "Wings on my shoulder, just like Chandler's, but much smaller. His started getting color added to it by an unseen force when he left for classes this morning. I was bored at home, waiting to see what else I got when I decided to come here."

"What else is on either of you?" She told her how Chandler had this crown on his upper abdomen. "And you? Do you have a crown as well? Where is it coming from, Sasha?"

"What we have been promoted to, I guess you could say. And yes, I have a nice crown as well. It's in the same place that his is. So that if we were standing toe to toe, even though he's taller than me, they would touch. The same with the wings. When I have my back to his chest, they touch there as well." Raven asked her what she thought they might mean. "We know what they mean. We were told about them last night. You should have seen us, waiting up all night for some unseen hand to start punching into our skin with little needles marring us up. It didn't happen that way. All we did was go to sleep, and they came over us."

"You're starting to freak me out a little. A lot, really. What do they mean?" Sasha got up and poured herself a glass full of bourbon. Then when she drank it straight down, like it was a glass of tea, she refilled her glass. "Sasha, please tell me what's going on."

"Just don't freak out more, all right?" Raven said that she'd try not to. "I guess that's about the best that I can hope for. The wings that Chandler has are to protect us. When we're touching our wings, even an atomic bomb going off will not harm us if he's wrapped around the two of us, and we're touching. He can also, sort of, fly. Not where you could see him, but in the ghost world, he can travel a great distance if he needs to look for someone. It will come in handy a great deal, I was told. I can't fly, but my wings will do so much more for children once they are in this family. Such as brush away sadness and sorrow, and protect them. They'll not have to suffer overly much about things that hurt their hearts or their bodies. Are you all right so far?"

"I think so. What happens to the rest of us? I mean, when disaster strikes, our children are safe, but we're to be shit out of luck?" Sasha shook her head. "Well, that's good. I'd hate to have to try and get under yours and Chandler's wings to be safe, so I can take care of my children." Sasha asked her not to joke about this. "It's joke about it or freak the fuck out, honey. Joking about it means I get to keep my dignity. Freaking out means that I'm a ball of sweat and messy shit trying to think this thing to its end. What else do I need to know?"

"Our crowns are there for all dead to see. The living

can only see them if we allow it. They were a little vague on why a human would need to know about that, but I was just trying to absorb as much as I could at the time." Raven nodded. "When we're surrounded by some dead—it needs to be more than four—the crowns that we have will glow above our heads like a beacon for them to know who is in charge."

"In charge of what? Or do I want to know?" Sasha told her that she was working up to that. "Okay, but I want you to know that the next time you have some real world shit to tell me, I like it all at one time. Rip the fucking Band-Aid off and tell me all about it. Okay?"

"Yes. Good to know. We're immortal." Raven nodded. "No. You nod, but we're all immortal. I don't know if we're true immortals or not just yet. I have some things that I'm still asking questions about. All of the Bishops, the family of the Bishops, as well as any children that come to us by heart or birth will be the same. No one dies."

"Okay, immortal. I understand the word, but I need to process this a little more. In the meantime, are there exceptions to this rule of yours?" Sasha told her that her mother and her family would need to be excluded from the family by telling them that they were no longer her family. "I need to tell my mother that she's not my family, and she dies when her time comes. Same with your mother and sister, I'm assuming. They just grow old and die like everyone else. I can live with that if you can."

"I can. They'd be trouble forever. I no more want that than I want you to ever be pissed at me. I think I can take you, but I don't want to have to figure it out." Raven just grinned at her. "Also, not only are we immortal, but we won't ever get sick. As it is now, you can heal quickly, but when you're sick, say from someone or something that poisons you, it will have no effect on you."

"Back to the immortal thing. When you say children of our heart, you're talking about children that we might adopt. Because I know for a fact that we both love Pip as if she were our own." Sasha told her that was correct. "Good. I like that. Okay, sickness. Not a sniffle? Or something like an ingrown toenail?"

"Nothing. No. However, I didn't ask about ingrown toenails, but I guess we can figure that out as we go. Do you get them often?" Raven told her that she'd never had one. "Me either. So I guess we can mark that one as a when-it-happens-we'll-know sort of thing. Also, and I didn't understand this until just this moment, once you tell a person that they are no longer a part of your heart and family, then you can never take it back. I asked about something with that, and you might understand it better than I do, but if a person is very ancient, say someone that has been around forever, once you tell them that they're no longer a part of the family, they are dead to dust." Raven leaned back in her chair. "You understand, don't you?"

"I think so. It would be like a vampire meeting the sun. They would just be gone to dust. That's pretty harsh. I don't know that the family has anyone like that hanging around, but I'd think that if my grandma would be around forever and someone said that to her, she'd just simply turn to dust as well. I think, just so there are no mistakes, children should never know that tidbit. I can see a child, pissed off because of something we're doing to keep them safe, saying that and killing off the family member that is there. Okay?"

"I agree. My goodness, I would never have thought of that one."

Raven watched as Sasha made a note in her notebook. She had thought that it was goofy that the woman had to write things down. However, once she started doing the same thing, making herself notes about other things that had popped into her head, she got more things finished in a timely manner. Raven noticed that Sawyer had started doing it as well.

"I have more information. Are you ready for it?"

"I think I am. Will we be marked like you are?" Sasha simply pulled Raven's wrist to her and moved up her sleeve. There was the tiniest little heart there that she'd ever seen. "This is all we'll get? I mean, it's sort of small for anyone to notice, don't you think?"

"When it's necessary, it'll be larger. I'm not sure how that works, but that's what I was told. Hailey, she's the ghost that is helping me, she said that she'd answer any questions that you all might have about anything pertaining to this."

Raven looked closer at the heart and saw that it wasn't just black, but a lot of colors. She supposed there was a reason for the colors, but something else popped into her head at that moment.

"This mark is on all of us, correct?" Sasha told her that she assumed so. "Right, another one of those things that we'll have to test it to be sure. I want you to go with me. I need to have a conversation with my mother. While there, if you want, I'll be with you when you tell your family. Deal?"

"Yes, excellent. You saved me from having to beg you to go. By the way, I've spoken about this with Sippy a little. Not as much as I have you, but she had the general idea. I don't think she's overly happy about the fact that someone did this without asking her. I think she just needs to realize the implications of what she's been gifted with. Like seeing her grandchildren grow up and have children." Raven said that she would come around, or they'd knock her around to it. "I think that she will without blows, don't you?"

"I do. And to be honest with you, I'm terrified of

Sippy. She has that quiet way about her that makes you think that she doesn't have all her marbles. But once she opens her mouth, you know that you've hit up on a shit storm that you're never gonna get cleaned up after." Sasha told her that she was very colorful at times. "Yes, well, I hang around men a great deal when I'm working. They tend to forget that I'm a woman and not one of the guys. In the business world, I'm top dog. When it comes to being gentle and understanding, I'm at the bottom of the list. I'm shadowing you in the ways of being a nice bitch."

"Thank you, I think."

Raven asked Molly and her grandma if they wanted to go with them. As the four of them loaded up in the car, Holly and Molly said that they'd wait for them in the car when they went to see the mothers. After that, Raven said they'd have a nice big lunch, as the guys were all busy.

"Also, I have to figure out some things about getting my shit together about how to take care of our house. I tried just running the vacuum this morning and nearly killed myself in doing just the upper floors. We have a staff, but I hate to bother them about just sweeping when I'm capable of.... Well, in a regular house, I'm capable of doing it on my own."

"Use the staff, Sasha. The people that are there are all the ones that I had when I lived there. You just ask them for something, and they'll bend over backwards in getting it done. They love working for the two of you. I still keep in contact with some of them." Holly laughed. "My goodness, now I know what Sherman meant when he said that you were looking to fire them all. I just couldn't for the life of me figure out what he was talking about. You'll have enough to keep you busy now that you and Chandler are married, and he's going to school and working."

"I will then. I didn't want them to think that we were taking advantage of them." Raven laughed and said that she loved to trip them up sometimes by asking for something outrageous. "They still came through for you, didn't they?"

"They really did. I will admit that here lately, I've been using the help a great deal more because I seem to be exhausted all the time. Sawyer told me that I'd get used to it. But I have to tell you— Hang on ladies, we're going to go and get Sippy. We need her on this outing as well." Raven did a U-turn, and they made their way to the farm. The house that Sippy and Saul had decided on was being built now. "I'm really glad that they decided to have a new home. And here. It'll still be like coming home for the guys, don't you think?"

"I heard they were having four extra bedrooms put in. For the children. I'm so jealous of that thought. I've decided to do the same, so I can have the kids over all to myself too." Raven looked at her grandma in the rearview mirror when she said that, her heart breaking that Grandma was moving out. "I'll be close, Raven. Sawyer and I have been plotting. I'm going to build back there on your property that butts up against the orchard. I'm excited about being able to have fruit whenever I want it."

After having to convince Sippy to come along with them, they headed to the jail. Getting it over with on an empty stomach seemed the way to go, especially since Raven was having so much trouble keeping food down, and Sasha had an excitable stomach. Raven would have to remember that, an excitable stomach. It was perfectly apt for what Sasha had, and a kinda nice way to say puking all the time.

~*~

Chandler decided that he loved being a vet more than anything else that he could have become. The fact that he'd had to put down a horse this morning didn't deter him from his passion. The horse was suffering, and the only way to make him better was to put him down. It was, he knew, one of the hardest things he'd have to deal with.

"I thought you'd be squeamish about that horse of Mr. Tailor's. You did that right well." Doc Joe had been with him all day, but he could see that the man was starting to wane a little. He'd never realized how old the man was until he told him today. He was nearing ninety. "I hope you'll let me finish here by saying that I'm going to leave you my practice, Chandler. My kids don't want it, and they surely won't know what to do with all the equipment I've collected over the years. Leaving it to you, they all agreed, is about the best thing this old man could do."

"I don't know what to say." He told him to say that he'd take it. "Yes, I will. I can't thank you enough for this. I mean, I never expected this."

"I know you didn't. That's what makes it all the nicer for me. I could see you turning down work close to here so that you'd not bother my practice. But I'm tired, and I don't know how much more of running around in the middle of the night I can take." They shook hands on the deal. "The only thing is that the building belongs to my great-granddaughter now, Penny. Her grandmamma Wendy owned it first. She had it in her head about twenty or so years ago that she wanted to have herself a nice little shop to sell her things. Don't know now nor back then what things she was thinking of selling, Wendy is about ten times the laziest person that you've ever met. I'm thinking that's why my great-granddaughter is so busy all the time. She doesn't want to be thought of as being like her father either, I'm guessing. Not that Wendy is a bad person or anything. But she'd rather sit around and watch television than to get out and be something. Those two boys of Wendy's are about as bad as their mother, I'm guessing. Tony is my great-granddaughter's father. James is Wendy's other son. Tony never married, but somehow he ended up with that child. Penny is making a name for herself too. She's a weaver. Never seen it done until she came along and gave me a quick lesson on it. Never seen the likes, I have to tell you."

"Is that the great-granddaughter that is getting married soon? I saw something about it in the paper." Doc Joe said that was the one. "Congratulations on that. I'm sure you're wanting great-great-grandchildren just like her."

"So long as they ain't a bit like Dutch. He's his mother's son, that's for sure. The lot of them are little shits. I think they're marrying into the family on account of them thinking that we're some kind of rich. We ain't. Penny has herself a nice nest egg, but she is far from rich. Dutch Donnelly, you know him?" Chandler told him that he didn't think he did. "You'd remember him if you did. He's not all that tall and has a gut on him like he drinks beer a great deal, as I'm sure he does. Straw hair. Not the color, but it looks like it's as soft as the crap is. He's got himself three brothers that are just like him, and he's got him a sister too. She's smarter than all of them put together. Don't have much to do with them either, I don't think. Her name is Emmie Donnelly."

"I think I heard of her. She's the new bank manager downtown." Doc said that was her. "It's a wonder they don't have her try and let them in the bank some night the way you talk about them."

"I'm sure that it ain't for lack of trying to get her to cooperate. Emmie and Penny, they're good friends last time I heard. But I think that there is a strain there with Emmie trying to get Penny to change up her mind on marrying her brother. I hope they can work it out and that Emmie can convince my great-granddaughter. There are more fish in the sea than a dumbass like Donnelly." Chandler laughed with Doc. "You tell me something there, son. You tell me why it is that people just don't pick out the right person for themselves. Martha and I, we had us a good life. Married nearly seventy years when she passed on. Yet there are folks out there that go into marrying with a chip on their shoulder and a prenup that says that if we don't work things out, you get shit, and I get to keep all my toys. Damn people. They should take a lesson from shifters like you and your family. Never met a family more in love with being in love in all my days. And that's a good long time if you ask me."

"As you said, I think that people—not all, but a large part of them—are going into things with their eyes closed. Or, more than likely, with their noses glued to their phones. They see online or wherever about how this or that marriage is working because of some stupid idea. Then they try it. When that doesn't work out, they just give up. I say that talking is the best way to make sure that things are out in the open. You know Raven, don't you?" Doc laughed and said that everyone did. "Right. Because when she has an idea or a problem, she gets to the heart of things. Today, she and my wife are going in to talk to their mothers. Now there is a group of nasty women. But they're going to tell them off, and when they're done, they're all going to have lunch together. It's done and over with them. My mom is learning to say what she thinks too."

"I bet that's a scary thing right there." Instead of answering him, Chandler just laughed. "You're a good boy, Chandler. Always have been. Why, when I saw you the first time, you were no more than about five or six years old. Brought me that old skunk telling me that I needed to fix him up. Never seen such an animal take to someone like that thing did to you. And it never once sprayed no one in your home either, I'm betting."

"No. Stinky—that was his name. He only had to protect me one time, and the bigger kids left me alone. I think that smell is still lingering a little on the Jefferson boys. I'd not thought of that in a long time. I used to bring you all kinds of things like that back in the day. Some you could save, others you helped me bury.

You're a good man, Doc." Doc thanked him, and they both watched as his dad pulled into the circular drive of the office they were both sitting in front of. "Dad? Everything all right?"

"Sure. I was wondering if you and the others—you can come along too, Doc—wanted to have us a nice dinner out tonight. The womenfolk, they've done their duty by their mothers, thank goodness, and now they're having them a blast at the restaurant in Columbus. Thought you all would like to join me for a steak dinner or something."

"Sure." Before they could make much more than some arrangements, the office phone rang. While he sat on the porch with his dad, Doc went in to answer it. "I was just reminiscing with Doc about the animals that I used to bring him. I can't believe that I've wanted to be this my entire life."

"I despaired every time your momma told me that you'd brought home another patient. I was always glad when I found out it was usually just a wee little thing." Dad asked him about his work. Chandler said he was having a good go at it. "I'm glad for you, son. I heard you had to put down one of Mr. Tailor's horses this morning. He's going to need some help come summer. Now that you're a married man, you not going to be helping out around town with your old man?"

"I don't think I'd want to anymore, Dad. Spending

time with a special man like you? What will people say about me?" They both laughed. "You know that all you have to do is call me and I'll be there. Even Sasha wants to learn how to drive one of the bigger tractors to help out. She thought that if Molly could do it, she could as well."

"No reason to think that she couldn't." Both of them stood up when Doc came out of the building. They could both see that he'd been crying. "What is it, Doc? What can we help you out with? Anything, you just name it."

"My daughter. Wendy. She's been killed." Doc nearly fell to the porch and would have had Chandler not grabbed him. "I was just talking to you about her, Chandler, and then she goes and gets herself killed. I know that I complained about her a lot, but I did love her to pieces. Her kids are going to be devastated for sure. The police told me that she was on her way back from the store when she was playing around on her phone and ran herself up under a semi. They know that was what she was doing because she was on the phone with the police when it happened."

"What was she calling the police for, Doc? Someone threatening her or something?" Chandler looked at his dad when he spoke. "Come on, Doc. I'll run you home. There ain't nothing going on around here that needs your attention. Chandler here will close up for you."

"Chandler, you don't mind, do you?" Instead of answering the elderly man, he helped him to Dad's truck. "I just don't know what I'm to do. The police said that I'd have to notify her kids on this. Wendy has her two kids, and then there is her brother and sister, Thomas and Cheryl. I have to call them. Will you stay with me, Saul, while I call them?"

"Of course, I will. Come on now. I'll even make you a bit of dinner." Doc mentioned their plans. "They was only plans, Doc. Nothing earthshattering. I'd much rather be with you than to be sitting around with a bunch of kids that don't have the sense to get in out of the rain sometimes."

Dad winked at him. Chandler knew what he was doing—making small talk while Doc thought through what had just happened. When they pulled away from the building, Chandler reached out to his family to let them know what had happened.

Oh, that poor man. Mom knew the entire family. Chandler thought that she would have. *Wendy wasn't a very good starter, her mother used to say, but she was a good mom. Her kids, they have kids too now that I think on it. I'll have to sit down to think about what their names are.*

Dad has gone to his house to help him make the calls. I'm here at the office, just waiting for five so that I can close up for him. Doc and I were just talking about his family when Dad pulled up to talk me into going out to dinner with him. I'm guessing that she went fast. She drove up under a semi or something like that, I was told. He shivered when he thought of what might have happened to the older woman as his mom told him that it was a terrible shame. *It'll be hard on them all.*

We should come home. Chandler said that there was no reason for that. There wasn't anything that any of them could do until the arrangements were made. *What do you think? Should we head back of just stay here? I don't really want to. I'm having a wonderful time with you girls. I know that Holly is as well.*

Like Chandler said, there isn't anything we can do. It's sad, but I don't think that any of us knew the family all that well. The guys might. Sawyer said that he and the others had gone to school with Wendy's children. *We'll stay here then. I, for one, after fighting with my mother, could use a good dinner out. Janet Stipple isn't going to bother me anymore after this.*

So they had made their peace with their mothers. Chandler was glad for that. It would go a long way in their long lives not to have to be on the lookout for one of them to come along and fuck things up for them. That was what Sasha had said to him before she'd left to see Raven. Chandler thought the two of them had gotten close, and was glad for it.

Sasha had told him before they left the jail that her mother was telling her that nothing would stick. Then when she was let out, they'd all be living with her since she'd called the cops on them. There was no way that Katie was getting out of jail. Ever. There were just too many charges against her to think that she ever would. And Pearl had made a deal with the Feds that had her telling things against her mother and brother.

At four-thirty, a little car pulled up in front of the building. Chandler was outside again, having gone in twice to answer a sales call. The woman who got out of the car had been crying, and he knew that she had to be related to old Doc.

"Do you know where Grandpa Joe is?" He told her how he'd gone home with his dad when the call had come in. "My grandma. Grandpa Joe shouldn't be alone, so I'm glad that your dad is with him. I'm Penny Harold. Wendy Harold is—was my grandma. You're…?"

"Sorry. Chandler Bishop. Your grandpa Joe is letting me work for him while I go back to school to become a vet." She nodded and looked down the main street to where the building was. "I'm so sorry about your grandma, Penny. If you need anything, just let me and my family know."

"Thank you. Will you please tell Emmie Donnelly that I've gone to my grandpa's home? I want to be with him before the others show up." Chandler said that he'd do that. "Thank you. If you don't mind, don't tell the others that I've arrived, nor that Emmie is with me. I need their drama right now like I need a hole in my head."

When she pulled away, not a minute or two later, Emmie pulled in and asked about Penny. After sending her on her way, it was five o'clock, and he closed up. If any of the other family members showed up, he didn't leave them a note to tell them where to go.

He was nearly home when he saw the Donnellys go by him in the opposite direction. He then realized that Penny didn't mention what to tell Dutch. He hoped that she was going to listen to Emmie and forget about the man, but it wasn't any of his business.

Going home, Chandler realized that he was going to be eating alone tonight. Reaching out to his brothers, he invited them to have dinner with him. The only one that couldn't make it was Wesley. He had a date tonight. However, it didn't sound like he was all that thrilled to be going on it when he said that if he got done early, he'd meet them.

Sounds more like a dental appointment than a date, Wesley. Were you set up on this thing? Wesley told them that he had been. *Well, have fun. We're going to be having dinner around six-thirty if you want to come by there before your date.*

I might do that. They were all laughing when Westley told them that this was a mistake and that the woman was nice, but he didn't have time for dating. *I have the last of the crops to bring in, and I don't have time to be sitting around with a woman that has marriage on her head. She actually told me that she hoped that things would progress quickly with us. She so loves a Christmas wedding. I should cancel.*

Yes, and do it now.

It was no longer funny. They decided that they were going to go to the same restaurant that Wesley had made reservations at, just in case. They didn't know this woman, but there was no way that she could be his mate if she was moving him forward this fast.

Chapter 10

Wesley wasn't able to get in touch with Rose personally, but he did leave her several messages. He told her that his brothers had invited him out and that he'd not be able to make their date. Wesley also told her that he'd be getting in early, so for her to leave him a message if she got his message after showing up at the place.

Rose Marie Conley was her name. He thought it was odd, too, that she'd told him repeatedly that if he wanted to get in touch with her just to call her cell. That was all she had, and she had it on her all the time. Now that he had time to think about what she'd said to him the other day when she'd asked him out, Wesley knew that she was more than just having a date with him. This woman was trying to get her claws into him.

He knew that what was going on was a little over

the top. She had asked him out, of that he was certain. Wesley tried to think how he'd even agreed to it. Rose had said they should go out sometime, and he found himself all of a sudden making plans to meet her at the restaurant. There wasn't even a pause in her saying that and him moving his plans around to make it happen.

Making the reservations for seven even sounded like nothing he'd have done. Christ, he was in bed by nine every night, so that he could get up at the crack of dawn to get his day going. Eating dinner at seven to go home and be in bed by nine didn't even occur to him until he walked into the restaurant with his brothers. The fact that they'd changed their plans to help him out made Wesley feel slightly better. But once he saw Rose in the restaurant ahead of even their early arrival had all kinds of warning signs going off in his head.

She was speaking to one of the wait staff when he was seated with the rest of them. Sawyer got up to speak to the staff member when Rose went to the ladies' room. Sawyer was really getting to know everyone in town, and this time Wesley didn't want to make fun of him about it but was ever so grateful for it.

"Hello, darling." He looked around when someone spoke, and he was surprised as hell that it was Rose. "Don't you have a kiss for me, Wes? I do hope you don't mind, but I've decided to join you all since you had to break our date because of them."

"No, I don't think so." Sawyer sat down as he was speaking. "We're here to have a good time, and I think you'd just rain on our fun, Rose. And he's Wesley, not Wes. He doesn't like to shorten an already short name. He never has."

"That was just rude. Are you going to allow him to speak to me that way, *Wes*? Wes, I really think you should say something to your brother about his manners too. That isn't very nice of him." Wesley pulled away from her running her fingers through his hair. "What's the matter, honey? You sure liked it last night when we were playing around."

"I've never met you before today. As for last night, I haven't any idea what you might be referring to." Wesley spotted the police coming into the restaurant and glanced at his brother. Sawyer nodded only once. "I've left you several messages today to let you know that I'd broken our dinner plans. I wish now that I'd thought better of them when you were making them. My family is very important to me, and we're having dinner tonight. Don't call me again."

The officer just stood behind Rose but didn't engage with her. Rose, however, had plenty to say.

"I guess that this is our first lover's spat. And here in front of your family. Wes, darling, did you tell them the news? You really shouldn't keep it from them for much longer. Especially with me carrying your baby and us having a lovely Christmas wedding this year. Come on, honey—*Wes*—tell them."

"I've never met you before today. And it's impossible for me to have fathered your child. You are carrying a baby, but anyone that knows me knows that there isn't any way that it could be mine. You'll have to try that on someone that is human." She laughed, then seemed to realize what he'd said and stopped laughing. She asked him what he'd just said. "Yes, not human here. If you're smart, which I'm beginning to think there is no way that you are, you'll walk away from this before you dig yourself in too deep. I'm not going to be a father to anything that you might have gotten yourself impregnated with."

"You are not going to leave me alone to deal with this baby, Wes. You made a promise to me, and I'm going to make sure that you keep your word." She pulled out a gun and put it to his head. No one moved, not even the officer who had pulled out her own gun. "You tell them what I said is true, or you won't be marrying anyone, dumbass."

"I don't know you. I have no idea what is wrong with you other than you're a little off your rocker. I'm not the father of your child, nor do I plan to marry you. You, lady, are insane." Wesley decided that this was as good as time as any to assert himself in showing her that he wasn't human.

Letting his cat take him, he snarled loudly when he felt the bullet hit him in the shoulder. Taking the woman down with him, he held her under him while the police, three of them now, started spouting off things that were going on. It took him a moment to realize they were calling their dispatcher. Sawyer was there with him as he was asked to move off the woman.

By the time they were able to leave the now closed restaurant, Rose had been arrested and taken away. He'd been able to shift and put on some clothes that he forever had with him. And his brothers were there with him the entire time. Nothing like family to have around when the shit started rolling in.

"She was planning this for a while. Rose is the same woman that called my house a few months ago, about the time that I met Raven. She tried to tell me about a date that we didn't have." Sawyer said that he was sorry that he'd not recognized the name sooner. "She told the waiter that you and she were planning this big event soon. That you were there at the restaurant to figure out if their venue was what you wanted in the way of a pre-wedding rehearsal dinner. Needless to say, no one believed her when Charlie told the staff what was going on. They called the cops on her, not me."

"How the hell did she think she could get away with this? And why did she want to marry me, anyway?

I'm a farmer, guys. Not the usual type of person that people scam like this." Chandler told him he thought it was the big tractor and the fact that Raven had money. "I don't. I mean, I have a few bucks in the bank, but not enough to plan a big wedding with a woman that I don't know."

Wesley was home and in his bed by ten. Later than usual, but it mattered little. He wasn't able to sleep, nor was he able to calm his nerves down enough for him to relax. Getting up when nothing was working, he went to the living room of his place and decided that he'd do some work. It was then that he found an old yearbook.

Like his brothers, Wesley had graduated from high school early. They all attributed it to having Mom homeschool them for the first five years of school. She had them working on lessons whenever there was a spare moment. Mom told them that the only way to succeed in life was to be smart enough to know what life was about. By the time he was ready to go to school like his brothers had, Wesley had tested out enough to be put in school as a senior. An entire seven years before he should have been.

The yearbook was Sawyer's, so he figured that it seemed to be about the right age that Rose would have been in it. She'd been a senior, she'd told Sawyer when she'd tried to scam him, so that was all he had to work on. Stretching his shoulder that he'd been shot in, he was happy that a simple shift had taken care of the broken bones that had occurred when the bullet entered him.

He found her picture, but the name under it was different. She was Rose, but that was her last name rather than her first. Sharon Rose, he knew, as did all his brothers. Sharon Rose had moved to their town when she'd been a teenager. She lived with her grandparents until she got to be too much for them to handle.

Sharon was a handful, he remembered now. But only a week after she'd been kicked out of their home, her grandparents—nice people, he remembered—were found dead in their home. Sharon was living there with their corpses, and they'd put her away when she admitted to not just killing them, but their animals too.

Wesley made notes to tell his brothers about her and was glad to know that someone was going to be watching her for a while. Wesley didn't know why she'd been out of the asylum, but he hoped that she'd be able to return. There really was something wrong with her.

Feeling better about why this person had targeted him and not a human, he made his way to his bed again. He laughed at himself when he realized that he'd made it when he'd gotten up earlier, and wondered if his mate, if she was out there, would think him an odd duck, as Grandpa Bishop used to call him. For a farmer, he'd been told, he was the neatest person Grandpa had ever encountered. Instead of being insulted, Wesley had worn it like a badge, that he was special.

The knock at his door, at three in the morning, had him reaching for his ball bat. He wasn't sure that he could ever use it on someone, but it was nice to have around when he was met with something that he wasn't sure of. Of course, he told himself, he was a cat, but there was no point in pulling him out when he could take care of whatever bothered him with a few pops on the head with the bat.

Opening the door, he realized that it had been raining. The person standing on the front porch was soaked to the skin. When she looked up at him, he knew that she wasn't there to hurt him. The way she'd been beaten up made him think that she'd had enough tonight.

"Come in."

She did, and stood there shivering when he went to get her some of the clean towels that he had just washed. Handing her two of them, he asked if she needed the police.

"Not yet. I mean, I should more than likely call them, but I'm not ready to admit defeat just yet. I'm Emmie Donnelly. My brothers are looking for me. I think I was able to talk my friend out of marrying one of my brothers." He helped her come into his living room and said he'd get her some tea. "You're very nice. I think that Penny would do better marrying someone like you."

He nearly tripped on his way to the kitchen. Two marriage proposals in one night. Instead of asking her to leave, he finished making the tea and brought it to her. With her coat off, he could see that she was injured as badly as he thought she had been.

"Do you need me to do anything?" She shook her head, then nodded. "What is it? I can lend you my phone if you need to make a call. Or I can take you someplace where you think you'll be safe."

"If you don't mind, I'd just like to sit here and lick my wounds for a while. I know that you're a cat. Your brother, Gunner, I think he knows me if that helps you. I just need a nap, a place that is free of my family, and this warm drink."

He didn't know what to think but did reach out to Gunner.

I know of her, but not her personally. However, I do know the brothers. Pieces of shit, all of them. He told his brother what she'd told him. *You should put her up if you don't mind, Wesley. She's more than likely gone through this before, and just needs to hide out. The others aren't too keen on their sister being smarter than them.*

Wesley told him that he'd put her in his room and watch out for her brothers. It wasn't like he was going to get any sleep tonight now. When he realized that she was asleep, he made sure that was all she was, asleep. He didn't want her having some sort of head injury and passing out from it.

After he covered her up with one of the many quilts that his mom had made, he went to the kitchen to make himself some tea. Tomorrow was going to be a very long day, and getting an early start on it might make it a little shorter. He didn't think so, but he could convince himself of that to make himself feel better.

Leaving her a note, Wesley made his way out to the fields to get the last of the corn in that he'd been putting off. He was going to go to his new home soon, the one that had been purchased by Sawyer and Raven, and he was looking forward to it. Mom and Dad had told him that he could continue being a farmer with their land if he wanted. He did, very much so. That was all he wanted to do. Wesley didn't want to grow any kind of new plants. He didn't foresee himself coming up with a new way to plant either. Just farming. And when he had plenty enough for himself to use from what he was growing, then he'd help out the other farmers around. It was tough being a farmer nowadays, and he tried to make it work the best he could for himself and others as much as he could.

As the morning wore on, Wesley began to feel much better. Not having a bit of sleep usually would have him dozing off at the wheel. But today he had renewed faith that he was going to get this pasture picked and that he'd be able to put his equipment to good use helping out around other farms.

By one, he was on the neighboring farm working. At five, when he usually told himself that he could go another hour, he was finally feeling the lack of sleep. Heading home, he didn't even pause at the door to see if he had any mail. Instead, he made his way up to his room and flopped on the bed. Wesley was out before his head hit the pillow.

~*~

Penny was on the phone when her Uncle James told her to get off of it. It was her cell phone, not the house phone, so she just turned her back. Christ, she hated doing this, but she guessed that if it was left up to her grandma's brothers, nothing would be done. James jerked her around when she started talking.

"What the fuck, James? The house phone is in the kitchen." He drew back to hit her—he'd done it before—and she drew her gun. "Back the fuck off. I'm not a little kid anymore, and a double funeral wouldn't be much more expensive than a single one. Go the fuck away and leave me alone. Or I'll put a hole in your gut that will take them hours to find with all the flab you got on you."

"You think you're so smart, don't you?" She just

walked away from him and let him keep talking. "You'll not be someplace where you can have that gun on you all the time, little girl."

"Yes, my name is Penny Harold. I'm trying to find out if you have my grandma's body yet. Her name is Wendy Howard. She was in a fatal accident yesterday." The funeral director, Mr. Benson, told her that he'd not gotten word yet that she'd been released from the morgue in Columbus. "Thank you. I'll be in with my Grandpa Joe as soon as you let us know to make the arrangements for her. I think that she might have set something up a while back with you, Mr. Benson."

"Yes, she did. And it's all paid for too. Your grandma took out one of those funeral policies that paid for her funeral when the time came. She paid on it monthly until she had it finished up." That didn't sound like her grandma at all, but she didn't tell him that. "You and your Grandpa Joe, when you get here, all you need to do is arrange for the time of the service. She didn't want anything extra. Just a graveside."

"Good, that will help us in making plans. Was there anything else that I should know before we get there, Mr. Benson?" He told her that everything, including her flowers, were all arranged. "Thank you. Like I said, we'll be there when we hear from you."

When she got off the phone, she went out on the deck to find Grandpa Joe. He'd been sitting there since she'd arrived yesterday, only coming in to go to bed. He'd not said anything, but he did nod when she told him something. Her uncles and brothers had shown up an hour ago. They were there with the Donnelly men right now, who had shown up yesterday.

Dutch was pissed off that Emmie had left without explaining herself. Penny would have left too if she could have. They'd all knocked Emmie around enough that she'd had to leave or they might well have killed her, as they were threatening to do. Emmie would be hiding now, and that was good for her. Someday, Penny would like to be able to keep her safe. But there had to be someone keeping Penny safe first.

Breaking it off with Dutch could have been better timed, but she didn't want to have to deal with his shit along with all the other things going on right now. Besides, she'd been planning it for a few days now, and when he'd shown up with his brothers, she told him what her thoughts were on the subject of them hitching, as he called it.

"What do you mean, you're not marrying me? Penny, I'm a catch. You should be happy that I'm willing to give up my bachelor life for you." Penny wasn't sure if he was kidding or not, so only told him again that she wasn't marrying him. "You have to have a better reason than you just don't want to, Penny. I'm not a man that likes to be truffle with."

"It's trifled with, and I told you that I'm sorry. But since we never had a date set up or even a ring, then that should be fine with our families." He told her that it wasn't all right with him. "Too bad, Dutch. I'm not going to marry you. That's the end of it. If you give me any shit, then I'm going to have to have you arrested. I'm too busy and too stressed to be putting up with your bullshit today anyway. I don't even know why I considered it in the first place."

"You don't have to stay faithful to me, Penny. I never planned on it with you. Hell, a man has needs, and I don't see you fulfilling mine." Shaking her head, Penny turned to walk away. He pulled her around just as her uncle had, and she drew her gun. "You sure are quick on the draw there. What are you going to do if I have something bigger than that?"

He made a crude gesture with his cock, and she pretended to measure it. Of course, it was then that her dad came into the room and wanted to know why she'd not be marrying Dutch. She told him what she'd been telling Dutch—she no longer thought it was a good idea to marry at all.

"Well, you're not going to be living with me when you're old and gray. I've raised you." He hadn't, but her grandpa had. Penny said nothing. "I'm going to get my momma's house, and you'll never be welcome there. Especially if you don't marry Dutch here like you promised."

"I never promised Dutch anything. He asked, and I told him that I would give him an answer someday. Well, I did. Today. Not marrying him might be healthier for him than being married to me. Because as surely as I'm standing here, I'd have to kill him before the wedding vows were said."

Sitting outside with her grandpa, she told him that she wasn't marrying. He told her good and that he loved her. She loved this man as much as she would ever love anyone and told him that.

"I hope you find yourself someone that you can love and that will love you back, child. There is no greater joy than being in love." Rocking in the chair, she asked him about her grandma. "She never loved anyone more than she did whatever project she was doing at the time. Wendy was a good mom, I suppose. But the more I think on that, I'm not so sure she was as good as I thought. Those boys of hers, Tony and James, they ain't worth the spit that it takes to seal an envelope up if you ask me. Your daddy still hitting you?"

"Not as much since I've started pulling out my gun rather than waiting for him to drawback. Uncle James too. If I ever have the chance to shoot him, I plan on hitting him where his brains are. Right in his ass." They both laughed. That was something that she had always enjoyed about Grandpa Joe, he'd let her be herself. "I spoke to Chandler yesterday when I went by there to find you. He seems like a nice guy."

"There's a good man. He has himself a wife now, and a little girl. That whole family is one you can depend on." He looked at her then. "If these men give you too much trouble, you go to the Bishops, Penny. It won't matter to them at all if it's dark as coffee or bright in the day, you find one of them and be safe for me. Promise me that. You tell Emmie that too."

"I will. And I promise." Grandpa Joe looked out over the fields as she told him what the director had told her about Grandma's funeral arrangements. "I didn't think she'd have paid it off."

"She didn't. I did it. I paid off the ones for your daddy and uncle too. I made the arrangements with Mr. Benson when your grannie passed on, thinking that I'd like to have it all done and paid for in the event that I was gone and you were left holding the bills in your hands. A parent is never to outlive their children, honey. Not at all."

"I'm so sorry, Grandpa Joe. My heart breaks for you." He nodded, and she hugged him. When her cell went off, she answered the call from Emmie. After hanging up, she told him where Emmie was. "She must have heard you or something. She's bedded down at the house of Wesley Bishop. She said that she was going to sleep there and then hide out in the morning.

She'll keep in touch with me."

"You don't tell them others. Not even your daddy. He'll tell them Donnellys sure as I'm sitting here." Penny agreed with him. "Also, I wanted to let you in on something. The house that your grandma was living in? There ain't gonna be nobody getting that but you. Your name is on the deed, just like those buildings and the one that I work in downtown. You paid for them, and there isn't any reason them meatheads should be getting anything. I'd not tell them today or even soon about it. They'll find out soon enough when they hear from the lawyer that I hired to let them know."

"Dad was bragging how he was going to be living in Grandma's house when this was done, and that I'd not be welcome. I wish I could see his face when he figures out that he's getting less than nothing from his mother's estate. She only had a place to stay because I provided her with it." Grandpa Joe told her that was all he had too. "Yes, but I love you. I only liked her. She was as mean as a rattlesnake, too, you know."

"I do. I'm sitting here thinking about all the things that I didn't want to think about. Like she wasn't one to hold down a job, not on account of her being lazy, but because she had herself a record." Penny knew that as well. "Penny, I'm thinking that we did you wrong somehow in not raising them better than we did."

"Don't say that, Grandpa Joe. Please, don't say that.

As Grannie used to tell me, I'm what I am because of the way I was raised. And living with you and her was the best thing that ever happened to me. My dad sure didn't seem to have a knack for being a good parent. He was a terrible person my whole life." Grandpa Joe said he didn't want to think about what might have happened to her had they not gone to his place that day. "You saved my life. You've always been there for me. Even after you spoke to him about how he'd left an infant only three weeks old in a crib for two days, he seemed to think it was all right that I lived. Like he had something to do with that."

"They're all good for nothing. I can see that now. My heart, it was making things seem a little better when I didn't want to see it. Now that it's sort of hitting me in the face, I see all kinds of things that I wish I'd done something about. It's too late for me to do anything, but you keep on your toes about them. I don't trust any of them." She said she didn't either. "I've given Chandler my practice. I signed it all over to him a few months ago. I knew that he'd be the best man for the job. He thinks my kids didn't want it when in truth, I've no idea what they would have done to it but run it in the ground."

The door opened behind them, and neither of them spoke. It was James again. He told her that she needed to get in the house and deal with them some dinner.

She just stared at him.

"Did you hear me? I need something to eat. Grandpa has plenty here for us to eat, and you're going to come in and fix it up." She told him to fuck off. "Well, you sure do have yourself a mouth on you when Grandpa Joe is around, don't you? Penny, I'm not shitting you. Get in here and make some dinner or else."

He stood there for several minutes until she got up. When James went into the house, she told Grandpa Joe they were leaving. He asked her where they were going as he stood up to follow.

"I'm hungry too. And since I have no intentions of feeding them all, you and I will go and get us something. I don't even care if it's the leftover pizza that I have in my apartment. We'll get something. All right?" They were to the car when she realized that the house might be a mess by the time they returned. "I'm calling in reinforcements for the house too. We'll stay at my place for a couple of days, and make sure that they're all out of the house so they won't burn it to the ground."

Grandpa Joe was laughing as they pulled out of the driveway. Pulling out her phone, she had him make the call and put it on speakerphone so that she could talk to them while she drove.

"Hey, Michael. I'm sure you heard about my grandma dying yesterday." He said that he had and that he was sorry. She and Michael had gone to school together. "I am as well. I was wondering if you could go by Grandpa Joe's house and make sure that it's locked up tight for him. He's going to be spending a few days at my place so that we can think. There are people there that don't need to be hanging around his home and stealing from him while he's down."

"Who's all out there?" She told him. "Good. I have an outstanding warrant for Dutch. I hope to Christ you're not really marrying him, are you?"

"No. I'm not. I have no idea why I didn't just tell him that straight out." Michael said that he'd take care of them. "Thank you so much. If you could go by there once in a while, I'd be happy."

"I was going to see if Wesley could go out there too. His place isn't too far from your grandpa's, so that should keep it safe enough. He'll tell that family of his, and it'll be as safe as a baby when Mr. Joseph returns." She thanked him for that. "I wanted to also tell you that in addition to the warrant out for Dutch, there is one for your daddy. I'll be taking them both in. They might not be able to make the funeral, just a heads up."

Thanking him again, she smiled at Grandpa Joe when he said good. After closing the phone, they pulled into the parking lot of the Jim and Jam. It was a bar, but they had the best fish sandwich she'd ever eaten. Grandpa Joe was walking a little straighter when they entered.

It was going to be a long few days, but she was hoping that it would be safer now that they had some kind of backup. Penny called Emmie to tell her what they were doing, and she said that she'd pass on joining them. She said that she was going to head deep into the woods for a few days. Whatever that meant, Penny was all for it. The safer, the better for them all, she thought.

Before You Go...

HELP AN AUTHOR

write a review

THANK YOU!

Share your voice and help guide other readers to these wonderful books. Even if it's only a line or two, your reviews help readers discover the author's books so they can continue creating stories that you'll love. Log in to your favorite retailer and leave a review. Thank you.

Kathi Barton, a winner of the Pinnacle Book Achievement award as well as a best-selling author on Amazon and All Romance books, lives in Nashport, Ohio, with her husband, Paul. When not creating new worlds and romance, Kathi and her husband enjoy camping and going to auctions. She can also be seen at county fairs with her husband, who is an artist and potter.

Her muse, a cross between Jimmy Stewart and Hugh Jackman, brings her stories to life for her readers in a way that has them coming back time and again for more. Her favorite genre is paranormal romance, with a great deal of spice. You can visit Kathi on line and drop her an email if you'd like. She loves hearing from her fans. aaronskiss@gmail.com.

Follow Kathi on her blog: http://kathisbartonauthor.blogspot.com/

Made in the USA
Coppell, TX
25 March 2020